# John Horn

## LEGEND OF A LUMBERJACK

Brenda M. Weber

PublishAmerica
Baltimore

First printing

ISBN: 1-4137-5211-X
PUBLISHED BY PUBLISHAMERICA, LLLP
www.publishamerica.com
Baltimore

Printed in the United States of America

This is fondly dedicated to one of the most important men in my life—my dad, Richard (Bud) Weber, for believing in me, never criticizing me and teaching me to never be afraid to voice my opinion, no matter how strong. Thanks for just being you, Dad. I love you.

-Dad in 1960-

This is also dedicated to one of the men who found John Horn's grave—Raymond Holmberg

-Ray Holmberg and John Horn's grave-

And to the spirit of John Horn, may he rest in peace

With this my second book, I find I have more people to thank—

The encouragement of my two friends who are like daughters to me, Heather MacGregor and Jean King, is constant. With never a dull moment, these two women have offered support when needed, understanding always. They have shared every exciting step with me, their ears always willing to listen. For two women who don't like to read, they have faithfully proofread for me and were always asking for more. Their confidence in me has been like a warm blanket. They are so appreciated.

Samantha Mitchell, for allowing me to capture her beauty and grace to portray Lily for the cover photo.

My friend Arvo Lyyski. He has more wisdom than all the dictionaries and encyclopedias put together. He is an endless supply of knowledge. The vessel never runs dry. There is not one question I have ever asked that he does not know the answer to, and amazingly, he is always right. One of the humblest and knowledgeable men I know. (The Highlander)

Valerie Hartman, my friend and favorite librarian, for all her encouragement and respect.

Lyle (Sinker) Sangraw, for loving me and for his help whenever I ask.

Joey Davis, for giving me permission to use his grandparents' names for the camp cook and foreman.

Shirley Demars, the daughter of Ray Holmberg, for allowing me to use his photo.

Daniel White of Portraits Plus, for my back cover photo.

My children and family, for their unconditional love and support, and for believing in me.

A special acknowledgement to Lynn M. Emerick and Ann M. Weller, co-editors of William S. Crowe's *Lumberjack: Inside an Era in the Upper Peninsula of Michigan*, for permission to use reference to lumberjack terms and lifestyle.

Other publications used for reference purposes: Lumberjacks and River Pearls: Memories of Manistique by Jack Orr and A Guide to the Indians of Michigan's Upper Peninsula by Russell M. Magnaghi for use in names, terms, dates and locations.

# Contents

# John Horn

## Legend of a Lumberjack

# INTRODUCTION

.

About the only thing anyone knows about John Horn is that he was buried along a branch of the Manistique River. He sleeps silently in the ground, deep in the forest of the Upper Peninsula of Michigan. He has never spoken from the grave to tell his story so I offer you my version of who John Horn was and how he came to be buried in a shallow grave of four feet.

John Horn was a real man who probably walked the streets of Manistique and through the forests where virgin white pine was king. He lived his life as a lumberjack over a hundred years ago. He may have been an immigrant or just a drifter. He may have been well liked or hated. He may have been a socialite or a loner who stuck to his own ways. He may have loved a girl or just dedicated his life to the forest. No one will ever know.

Some years ago a ballad was written about John Horn, another rendition of who he was. Ballads are sentimental narratives while legends are unauthenticated stories from earlier times, preserved by tradition and thought to be historical. Either way, John Horn deserves to be recognized, even though recognition can only be assumed.

If John Horn could speak from the grave I think he'd be happy with this rendition of him. I think he'd be flattered to be thought of as a legend, to know that people still speak of him and visit his grave year after year. John Horn will never truly die as long as people keep him alive by speaking of him and honoring his spirit.

Living in the Upper Peninsula of Michigan is an adventure all in itself. People from the cities visit us here, and comment on the serene lifestyle, fresh air, the solitude and the sense of being in God's country. We natives are aware of the beauty and appreciate our simple lifestyles. We take nothing for granted and are thankful for the gifts bestowed upon us by the natural beauty that surrounds us.

Many stories are told and re-told of our historical Upper Peninsula. We hear stories of fur trappers and traders, gangsters as famous as Al Capone and lumberjacks such as Paul Bunyan who walked our lands. This is the story of another lumberjack who left behind nothing more than a name on a wooden cross and a shallow grave in the middle of nowhere.

You are going on a journey, my friend, of both present and past and you will come to know and love the legend and the man John Horn.

# GRAVE MARKER

They stumbled across the grave while they were hunting in an area known as the flood woods along the Manistique River. The brothers had walked many times along the high banks and ridges. They thought they knew everything there was to know about the heavily wooded areas in the forest. They had explored every turn, bend and twist of the endless snaky river. They could name every tree in the forest—white pine, jack pine, red pine, hemlock, cedar, birch and maple. They knew every wild flower—trillium, wild violets, forget-me-nots, jack-in-the-pulpit, wild iris. They often made a game out of seeing which one could get the others lost. They never used a compass; the forest was that familiar to them. They claimed to know it like the backs of their hands.

Now, on this particular hunt, they rounded a bend in the river and came upon a roughly hewn wooden cross, barely visible in the deep underbrush. In fact, they would have missed it if Grant hadn't lost his footing and stumbled to the ground. The cross was embedded deep into the ground, leaning sideways, almost touching the ground like a wounded soldier. Engraved into the hardwood in deep grooves that released the spirit of the wood were these simple words: John Horn—April 1897. It was 1960 and the grave was already over a half century old. After years of exposure to every element Mother Nature exhibits, under layers of encrusted moss dried with age, they had found a bit of history. The trouble was, this bit of history was situated on a wide bend and the banks were about to be washed away into the majestic flow of the Manistique River.

With each new spring the ice would break up on the river. The melting snow from upriver would fill the river, sometimes beyond its capacity. There were years when the water would crest, causing the river to flood. The raging water would come crashing and splashing with such force that it would spare none of the dirt, sand or tree roots in its path, often sending the trees attached to the roots sliding ungracefully into the deep rushing water. Those trees uprooted would be towed along in the raging waters until they would become lodged on a deadhead log or get held up on another fallen tree. The force of the water slamming into the banks would pummel the sand like a giant fist, causing the base to weaken until finally the top portion of sod would succumb to inevitable erosion.

With their discovery the brothers experienced the eerie sense of stepping back into time. They felt reverence for the soul buried beneath the earth so many years ago during one of the many years in which the lumberjacks reigned. They assumed he was a lumberjack—who else would be buried in the middle of nowhere, in a forest so thick with trees the earth rarely saw sunlight? Because this lonely soul rested along the riverbank they figured he was buried on the spot, perhaps after dying on a log run. They knew they had stumbled upon holy ground and, showing respect for the dead, they removed their hats. Even the birds stopped twittering as the forest became still. A soft whispering breeze placed a kiss of warm breath on their cheeks.

After being touched by John Horn's spirit they had to face the dilemma of what to do to save his grave from being washed into the river. The grave may have at one time been fifty or sixty yards away from the river's edge, but that was sixty-three years ago, and now today it was about three feet from the edge. With each passing year the riverbank would lose more ground from being washed away at the mercy of turbulent waters. The brothers calculated that in another three to four years John Horn's remains would be forever lost, as he too would be forced to unceremoniously slide into the river. His worm-eaten body and brittle bones would be uprooted from his happy hunting ground and perhaps release a spirit of discontent into the solemn setting the forest offered.

They decided to ask some questions in town and after approaching the right people, they would make a decision as to what could be done. They wanted to move the grave, but knowing it might be considered illegal, they weighed the consequences. They realized it might be considered grave robbing or something far worse, something morbid in nature. If the wrong people found out they could even end up in jail. They wanted to do everything possible to avoid that and more importantly avoid a bunch of people, curiosity seekers, learning of their discovery and infiltrating their neck of the woods, so to speak.

Their first step was to check the death records at the local courthouse. They found a death record for one John Horn, April 17, 1897. There was no record of his birth. They also learned from historical records that only five men had lost their lives on log runs in the days when the great white pines were being cut and milled in Manistique. The Chicago and Weston Lumbering Companies employed twelve to fifteen hundred men. Seventy-five of them were Indians, and John Horn was one of them.

They made some inquiries and learned it only takes one burial to establish a cemetery, thus reinforcing their belief that there might be legal ramifications if they moved this grave. It would be considered grave robbing. They told one of the workers in the records department what they had found and the danger of losing the grave to the Manistique River. They were told, in no uncertain terms, that under no circumstances could they move the grave.

When the brothers left the courthouse they knew what they had to do and they were determined to do it—save John Horn's grave. They decided not to tell anyone where the grave was located; they would keep it in the family. They would just go back up into the woods equipped with the proper digging tools and dig up John Horn, move him a safe distance back from the river and give him a second proper burial. Once it was done, no one could ever prove it and the brothers wouldn't bother to argue the point with anyone.

In digging up John Horn they laid out a large piece of heavy felt adjacent to the grave. They took precise measurements as they dug, recording the length, width and depth of the grave. As they unearthed his remains their nostrils picked up the musty odor of the damp dirt. Earthworms, white grubs, ants and centipedes had made this grave their home. They transferred his skeleton onto the canvas in the exact position he had rested in for so many years. There were no airtight caskets back then, only pine boxes, but John Horn did not even have the luxury of a pine box. His body had been wrapped in a piece of canvas, placed in a shallow grave and buried with perhaps a few simple words.

They discovered parts of his heavy trousers. One pocket contained five pebbles. They figured this was symbolic of his heritage or perhaps used to create saliva by being placed under his tongue on extremely hot days in the forest. Tucked into a tattered pocket of a nearly disintegrated twilled cotton work shirt was a portion of a cheap pocket watch. The face of it was nearly worn away. It was beyond any ability to read the numbers. It didn't matter anyway. Time had stopped for John Horn, suspended in an era which was now as dead as he was. His leather-calked boots with brass lace hooks were still intact. Inside one of his boots was a tiny gold wedding band. It was small enough to fit a child or a very petite woman. Why it was inside his boot would not be known until years later, when I would discover the mystery. John Horn was not a very tall man but he was large boned, and he must have been as strong as an ox to have worked on a log run. There was a good strong set of teeth in his head so the brothers figured him to be a younger man.

Because of his calked boots they knew he must have been a river driver. This was the toughest job in the days of the lumberjacks. A man had to be adept and sure footed to be able to ride the logs down the Manistique River. It was the highest paid job and the experience had to go with it. They were beginning to feel a kinship for John Horn. The brothers knew a loyal lumberjack lived and breathed the forest. He must have died an honorable man.

It took hours to measure, dig, move and lastly re-bury John Horn, but finally their task was complete. Everything was as it had been; only now, this lone lumberjack was a much safer distance from the river and would be assured of his final resting ground for hundreds of years to come. They shared a wonderful sense of patriotism and had no qualms about their good deed.

Bud, one of the brothers, had taken the time to construct a gravestone to be erected on the site. He had molded out of concrete a typical tombstone with the rounded top. It was about two feet high, maybe a foot wide and five inches thick. In the center was a round brass plate which he stamped with the same words found on the wooden cross—John Horn, April 1897. He added some of his own: Young and Brave.

As they completed their work they reverently bowed their heads and repeated the 23$^{rd}$ Psalm. "The Lord is my shepherd, I shall not want. . ." over the long dead Indian lumberjack. With the sweetness of the Lily of the Valley heightening their senses they placed a few wild flowers on the fresh mound of earth. They left John Horn to the serenity of the forest while a blue jay's shrill cry was heard in the distance. It was almost as if his spirit was thanking them, not only for their kindness and sensitivity but also for their great respect for the dead. They walked away hearing the silence of the grave.

The brothers vowed to return every year on Memorial Day. His spirit would live on in each of them and their families. It would become their family tradition to acknowledge this soldier of the forest with their solemn thoughts and kindred gestures. This tradition would indeed live for many years to come, with their families placing flowers and saying a prayer over the grave of John Horn.

# CEMETERY VISITS

The first recollection I have of John Horn is traipsing through the woods with my dad in 1965. There was a group of us, both kids and adults. We zigged and zagged around trees, ducked our heads under low branches, stepped over fallen trees, sidestepped stumps, jumped over or walked through rippling creeks, up and down ridges, literally weaving a confused path through the thick woods of the Manistique Forest. At times, some of the smaller kids were carried piggyback or on the shoulders of adults. All I knew was that we were going to visit someone named John Horn.

We came to a clearing at the side of the riverbank. I could see the river was at a low point. We made our way down the bank and began taking shoes and socks off, rolling up pant legs and wading into the river toward the opposite side. This was getting to be fun. The trek through the woods had taken some time and it was hot. The icy water felt soothing and refreshing on my pent up feet and the slimy mud slithering through my toes was a familiar and loved feeling.

As we forded the river we began climbing up the steep bank, which was a feat because we kept losing our footing as the sand kept sliding downhill under our feet, causing us to dig deeper while still losing ground. We finally clamored up onto firm ground and found ourselves in another clearing. There, in the middle of the clearing, was a lone tombstone. Shhhh—everyone was hushed and stood with mouths agape at this solitary site. Some had been here before while others had not. We began to gather wild flowers and leaves to place on this grave. We were told by one of the adults this was where John Horn was buried. Someone asked why he was way out in the middle of the woods all by himself. My dad answered, "He died way back in the 1800s and he was a lumberjack who fell off a log and drowned. Back then, they were buried where they died, and this is John Horn's final resting place."

We quietly and respectfully stood around the grave, bowing our heads while someone repeated the 23rd Psalm: "The Lord is my shepherd, I shall not want. . ." After placing our floral tokens on the grave we silently walked away, but I had to look back just once. I didn't want to leave John Horn all alone in this vast wilderness. One of the adults yelled for everyone to come on. We jumped down the riverbank, back into the water and made our way back through the woods to God's Lost Acres, my dad's hunting camp. I never understood how we made that long confusing expedition through the forest and came out exactly where we had started. I know no one carried a compass.

I was ten years old when I made the journey through the woods with my dad, aunts, uncles and cousins. Our families had made the journey before although I don't remember it. Each year on Memorial Day since 1960, my family had made this ritualistic excursion through the woods to visit John Horn's grave. It had been a family tradition from the time his grave was first discovered.

At ten years old I had a fixation about death; my mother had died the year before and I could still feel her presence around me. I felt a deep serenity and safety around cemeteries. I spent a great deal of time walking through the cemetery near my home. I often just sat under a tree amidst the gravestones, some old and decrepit from years of exposure to the elements. I remember feeling calmness within my soul as I would read and examine every tombstone. I would try to envision the people when they were alive, making up stories in my head of how they lived and died. Sometimes I would just sit in the cemetery and read a book or write poetry.

One particularly small gravestone had a lamb on the top of it. It was the grave of a baby. The only words on the flat surface the lamb rested upon were Baby Rebekha—1895. I found a flaw in the texture of the stone. When the sun hit it just right, it looked like the lamb had a teardrop under its eye.

I sensed in some unexplainable way I was a comfort to the souls that were long dead and buried. Sometimes I found myself talking aloud to unknown occupants of the graves, especially the babies, not wanting them to be alone, the way I felt. I never saw spirits or actually communicated with any dead people, just felt intimate with the empty air of the cemetery. I never thought it was morbid, and still don't. Cemeteries are fascinating to me, especially ancient ones.

After my initial awareness of visiting John Horn's grave, each year came to mean more to me than the previous. I found myself feeling hollow after I visited his grave. That feeling was a proverbial one to me. There has always been a definite emptiness within me since the death of my mother when I was at such an impressionable age. I always felt like I was a drifting soul trying to find my wayward way to where I truly belonged. As I grew older, for some strange and unexplainable reason I felt as if I belonged with John Horn. I felt like I had known him in another lifetime, but I knew that was impossible.

Over the years I've wondered about John Horn. What was he really like? How did he live? How did he die? Whom did he love? So many questions I wanted answered. I wanted to go back in time and find him, wanting to see if perhaps I really did know him and belong with him. I've never believed in reincarnation but have always felt a sense of longing to be somewhere else, somewhere safe and familiar to me. Feeling as if my life had taken a wrong turn, it seemed I had ended up in a time where I didn't really belong. When I die I want my ashes spread by John Horn's grave. I feel that is where I belong.

I never thought for a moment I would ever really know John Horn, but now I can say that I do. The circumstances in which this came about are both peculiar and bewildering to me, something created from a mixture of magical circumstances and mystical coincidence. I never would have dreamed in a million years the poetry I wrote about John Horn would come to life. Like rising mist from the shallow grave, his spirit would seek me out and capture my essence with his.

# POETRY CONTEST

I've written poetry since I was fifteen; gathering maturity has brought deeper thoughts, and thus more intense poetry. I've often dreamed of someone setting my poetry to music and someday hearing a famous country singer croon my words in a beautiful rendition of the song. I have entered some poetry contests over the years, received a couple of certificates of recognition, had one published in an anthology and I enjoy the self-satisfaction of finding graphic art for my words. Until recently I haven't really done too much of anything with my poetry other than share it with people I care about. Whenever I send in a poem to some new contest I always think, "Right, nothing will come of this." I've always thought that, until now.

I entered the contest in May of 2003. I had picked up a newspaper someone left behind at the Laundromat. The small ad quickly caught my eye: Poetry Contest. It was at some unheard of college in a small town in the middle of nowhere, but was open to the public. There was no entry fee, the poetry would be judged by one of the staff, an English teacher by the name of Emma Simms. No monetary prize was involved, just publication in the college newspaper and the local papers. *Why not*, I thought. It sounded like something I could do and I had the perfect poems to use. It had to be a series of correlating poems but no more than four in the series and at least two. I immediately thought of the poems I had written about John Horn, my personal image of him and his love for a girl named Lily. John Horn was real, but these were my renditions of what might have been. I submitted the two poems, and I'll share them with you.

## The Legend of John Horn

Gentle breezes whisper his name
With no one there to hear
The pine trees are his refuge
The river's force runs near
In the booming days of long ago
A forlorn drifter came to town
Young and brave, strong and free
No man could put him down
He wore his hair black and long
The wind cracked it like a whip
He carried himself tall and bold
A Colt-45 at his hip
People knew him as John Horn
A loner set in his ways
Camped out along the river
In the fearless lumberjack days
He soon jumped on a log run
With men grizzly and mean
He rode the raging river
Like no man had ever seen
A storm was brewing up above
Spring thaw was not complete
The mighty timber and gallant men
Now got the chance to meet
With desperation and chunks of ice
John Horn rode it down

But the logs jammed and shifted
When they reached the river's crown
He was thrown into the water
And felt its icy bite
With the fierceness of a giant
He fought with all his might
They buried him that day
A wooden marker, a shallow grave
Here lies John Horn
Young and brave

This was how I envisioned the Indian lumberjack who rested in the Manistique forest. I also thought there had to have been a woman he loved. The forest floor is covered with a blanket of trillium in the springtime. We call them wood lilies, so I named her Lily and this is her poem.

## The Legend of the Wood Lily

He had a wild and free spirit
No woman could tame
She knew when she saw him
John Horn was his name
His eyes blazed with fury
The wind whipped at his hair
She stole a quick glance
Just this once did she dare?
From under her lace bonnet
He caught a glimpse of blue eyes
She was the one they called Lily
What a pleasant surprise!
Skin as white as the pure driven snow
No end to the braid in her hair

She smiled at him with rose petal lips
Oh to kiss this one—beauty so rare
They planned for a rendezvous
At Weber's Spring off the creek
Each night in the moonlight
Their resistance grew weak
Their passion raged with wanton desire
And he called her his flame
The rebel and the preacher's daughter
Their love was forbidden
But there was no shame
On a blanket of forget-me-nots
They slept in the warm summer air
Naked bodies were gently covered
With the softness of her yellow hair
Their passion and love grew
But they were never discovered
Through the changing of seasons
They remained secret lovers
Then in early springtime
Came the news of his death
Her hand on her belly
His name on her breath
With mournful tears she said good-bye
At the spring and then at the river
She's carrying your baby, John Horn
Her father will never forgive her
Lily left town that day
But no one ever guessed
Soon after with a blanket of trillium
The lonely forest was blessed
People never saw such beauty
Petals as white as the pure driven snow
With a pistil like a braid of yellow
So much like Lily, you know

Now in the springtime in a tranquil forest
In the land where new life is born
You'll hear the wood lily whisper soft
I'll always love you, John Horn


I sent the poems off in an envelope marked "Poetry Contest" and never gave it much thought until I received a phone call in August from a woman named Emma Simms. I had forgotten she was the English teacher responsible for judging the contest. When she refreshed my memory I got excited; I thought I had won the contest and would have another published piece to my credit. She apologized for my first reaction, informing me I had not won but she had some questions about the poems I had submitted.

I thought it was a little strange but was willing to humor her. I thought it was even stranger when she asked if I would be willing to see her in person. I started thinking she was some kind of weirdo. She didn't want to go into detail over the phone and assured me she was harmless. She sounded very sincere and convinced me of the importance of our meeting. I agreed to meet her in a public place at a designated date and time.

# MEETING EMMA

We met at a coffee shop halfway between Manistique and the Mackinaw bridge. The first thing I noticed about Emma Simms was she was a very striking woman. I thought she was probably middle- aged but looked about ten years younger. I caught a whiff of her perfume, Jasmine. Her blonde hair was fixed in an upswept makeshift bundle on top of her head. Tendrils escaped here and there, giving her a look of being disheveled in an organized way, like the English teacher she was. She was dressed in blue jeans and an oversized sweater and was carrying a black portfolio. Her high-heeled boots made her appear tall and slender. She had an easy smile overflowing into her sparkling blue eyes and crinkling her pert nose. There was something about her eyes that made her seem familiar to me, as if I knew her from somewhere. I had never heard of Emma Simms before the poetry contest. I knew I had never laid eyes on this woman before in my life, but I still couldn't shake the feeling that I knew her from somewhere. Maybe it was an unexplained case of déjà vu.

We greeted each other with a casual handshake and sat down at a table in the back to guarantee our privacy. She ordered coffee and I ordered a can of soda with a glass of ice. We made small talk about the weather and her drive. She had been in Mackinaw City visiting relatives.

She commented on the beauty of the Upper Peninsula of Michigan. She had never been above the bridge and was surprised at the lakeshore, so many trees and the fresh air. She planned to take many pictures before she returned home. She would be spending the night at a motel. The waitress delivered our drinks and sensing we wanted privacy did not pressure us to order anything.

Emma's portfolio was on the table beside her and I kept glancing at it, wondering what was in there and if she planned to show me. She caught my glances and finally reached for and unzipped the case. First she withdrew a manila envelope, the one I had mailed my poems in for the contest. She smiled and said, "I want you to know, I love your poems."

"Thank you!" I said, and returned her smile.

"You're probably dying to know what this is all about, aren't you?"

"Well, yes, if I didn't win the poetry contest and you aren't offering to turn my poems into music, I am pretty curious why you would want to see me, so before I go crazy wondering, please tell me!"

Emma chuckled and said, "Before I tell you, I want to know how you came up with the idea for these poems, and more importantly, how did you come up with the name John Horn?"

I replied, "John Horn is a real person, a lumberjack who died in the late 1800's. My dad and his brothers found a grave in the woods by his hunting camp back in 1960…"

I proceeded to relate to Emma the details of their finding his grave, moving it away from the riverbank and the yearly ritual of my family visiting and placing flowers on his grave. She listened intently and I noticed a lump in her throat and a glistening of tears in her eyes, those haunting blue eyes of hers. I realize it is a touching story and may be hard to believe, but she seemed more enraptured than most people who had heard the story. Then it dawned on me. I thought I knew why she had come to me.

For years a woman from the Historical Society had tried to get my dad to take her to John Horn's grave. She wanted to write a story about it and document the whereabouts of the grave. My dad had always made one excuse or another, not wanting to take an outsider to the site and destroy the harmony of the forest cemetery of one. He feared it would turn into a circus of tours with an easily accessible manmade path. He swore he wouldn't let that happen. My thought was that this woman from the society had contacted someone from the National Historical Society and by some twist of fate it turned out to be Emma Simms, an English teacher who was judging a poetry contest. That might be a nearly impossible coincidence but it was rattling around in my head. I had laid John Horn in her lap, so to speak.

"Are you from the Historical Society?" I asked.

She laughed again and said, "Oh no, nothing like that."

"Okay," I said. "I can't stand it anymore, just tell me who you are and what this is all about, please!" I was getting ready to actually scream from the anticipation.

Emma laid my poetry aside and brought out another manila envelope. This woman was going to kill me with her methodical manner. She had an air of eccentricity with a hint of monkey business. I wondered if she was toying with me. I felt like I was on a game show, waiting to see what was behind a curtain. I wanted to reach across the table and grab the envelope, spill the contents onto the table and be done with it. This woman had to be one of the weirdest people I'd ever met, besides myself. If she wasn't a nutcase, I was, for sitting there with her.

I decided to pull myself back a bit. I sat back in my chair and crossed my arms across my chest. The top half of my body had been nearly draped across the table. Was I licking my lips and gritting my teeth? I couldn't stand the suspense but I was getting sick of this woman playing ping-pong with my emotions. I thought I'd try some reverse psychology with my body language and appear to distance myself from wanting to see what Emma had to show me. It worked.

She slid three photographs from the envelope. I noticed they were a little creased and yellowed with age. She laid them out on the table between us, facing them in my direction. I could tell they had been taken in the 1800s. They were black and white, leaning toward a sepia tint. One was a portrait of a young girl who looked amazingly like Emma. She had that same something in her eyes. I still couldn't grasp what it was. It was something uncanny but so subtle I couldn't put my finger on it. I didn't know if it was the look in their eyes, the shape of them or just something momentarily flickering in the back of my mind, just out of reach.

The girl had blonde hair like Emma, only hers was fixed in two thick braids wound together on top of her head. I could tell by the thickness her hair must have come to her waist or longer. She looked to be about seventeen, but had a maturity in her youthfulness. She looked innocent but also womanly in a respectful way. I flipped the picture over and almost fell off my chair when I read what was written on the back— "Lily at age 17." I felt my heart leap into a jumpstart, sending it racing to my throat. Had I crossed over into some kind of twilight zone? All I could do was look at Emma as I picked up the second photo.

This one was of two young men standing in the doorway of a very large house. A sign hung over the door, reading "Ravenwood." Back in the 1800s there had been a boarding house in Manistique called Ravenwood. My thoughts were whirling now, was this picture taken in Manistique? The sun cast a shadow across one of the men. His face wasn't visible enough under his wide brimmed hat to tell what he looked like but it didn't matter. The other one had jet-black hair hanging past his shoulders, penetrating black eyes and he was exceptionally handsome. He had broad shoulders, muscular arms and a very proud and bold look on his face. He was holding the reins of a stunning horse and he looked to be part Indian. My hands were trembling; my heart was thumping so loud I thought the whole place could hear it. My mind was racing as my thoughts began to bounce around like pieces from a rubber jigsaw puzzle. I was trying to catch the pieces to put together the complete picture but my common sense was telling me to throw my thoughts out the window.

This just could not be, but I knew what I would see as I flipped this second picture over—" John Horn at age 21."My hands were still shaking as I turned the photo back around and looked into the face of the man—John Horn. He looked exactly as I had envisioned him. Tears sprang to my eyes now and the lump in my own throat was extremely painful. This was the most bizarre thing I'd ever experienced in my life.

By this time I was close to hyperventilating and Emma was just sitting there with that look in her eyes and a smile on her face. I finally managed to stammer, "Where—where did you get—get these pictures?" My mouth was agape and my head was getting fuzzy. I kept thinking she really was from the Historical Society. She had found out about this, done some research somewhere, and this was all just a big coincidence. It was all just too weird! That did not explain how John Horn turned out to be the exact image I had cherished in my mind all these years. I didn't believe in anything weird like reincarnation, but maybe I should have.

Emma silently picked up the third photograph and handed it to me. I fought to make some sense out of all this. I had written two poems and had literally brought the characters to life. I knew John Horn was real, but how could I know what he looked like? How could I know there really was a Lily? By now it was obvious the two had been connected even if Emma still hadn't said more than two words since she brought the pictures out.

The last photo was also of Lily. Although she was a few years older now, I could tell it was the same woman. She was sitting on a fainting couch with a young girl at her side. They were dressed alike in white high-necked lace dresses with pearl buttons and long sleeves puffing out at the shoulders. There were more pearl buttons on the forearm. They were posed a bit sideways but shoulder to shoulder with their faces turned toward the photographer. Lily's hair was in an upsweep much like Emma's style and the little girl wore hers long, curled and pulled to one side over her front shoulder. I guessed the little girl was about seven or eight. They looked alike, aside from the little girl's hair. It was jet black, in conspicuous contrast to Lily's blonde hair. The little girl's eyes looked to be the same color as Lily's eyes. Even in the black and white photo their eyes were light and I assumed blue. They were both smiling but the little girl's expression made it almost possible to hear her giggling.

Of course I turned this photo over too. On the back was written—"Lily at age 29, Emily at age 7." It was probably safe to assume they were mother and daughter. I looked up at Emma, waiting to hear what she had to say about these photos, these people, and this weird zombie-like state I was sinking into. A sudden thought crossed my mind and I looked back at the photo I still held in my hands. Yes, there it was in Emily's eyes, that same look! *What was that look they had about them?* Lily and Emily both had that same unique look in their eyes and I just couldn't grasp what the similarity was. It was the same gnawing sense of familiarity that had first struck me about Emma. It was a faint strumming in the back of my mind, a low melodic strum of an ancient lyre. But what the hell was the tune?

# EERIE PHOTOGRAPHS

Emma must have sensed I was getting irritated by her lack of response to my spoken and unspoken questions, and I had so many questions. I wanted to start tossing them around, literally throw them at her, but I refrained, I would be patient. Emma just looked at me and said, "My mother just died last year, her name was Amber. All these photographs were kept in a box in her chest along with some other documents and my family tree. My grandmother's name was Emily and I'm named after her. Lily was my great-grandmother. As far as I know, Lily was never married but she gave birth to Emily in 1898 when she was twenty-two years old. Emily's father was John Horn."

An ant-crawling chill ran along my neck. I could feel icy goose bumps start to form on my arms, tiny spiders with sharp straight pins for legs, the eeriest feeling. This was more than déjà vu. This was more like being transported into someone else's life. I was sitting with a woman who was a descendant of a man who was long dead, yet I knew what he'd looked like, never before seeing his picture until now. Emma was a descendant of a woman I had made up in a poem, even the name I had given her was her actual name. My description of her features matched the photo, blonde hair and blue eyes. This was too weird even for me.

I suddenly felt I was in a dream trying to fight my way to alertness through the fog of the mysterious realm between sleep and wakefulness. I was so totally stunned I was motionless, speechless and practically senseless. This was something so completely bizarre it couldn't possibly be real, but it was, and I knew it. It took me a full ten minutes to clear my head, enough to try to make sense of it all. I could see Emma patiently sipping her cup of coffee. The waitress came once to fill it as I sat incoherently shocked, mumbling something about my soda being fine. The waitress scurried away, no doubt wondering about the weird lady at table five.

Emma produced a yellowed piece of paper, her family tree. I automatically took it from her hand with a sense of knowing what I would find, something else too peculiar for words. I had no idea just how uncanny things were until I started reading. It was a simple and sketchy line of ancestry. John Horn, born 1873—died April 17, 1897; Lily Abrams, born 1876—died May 24, 1955; Emily Abrams Horn, born 1898—died during childbirth, 1918; Amber Abrams Horn, born October 30, 1918—died July 20, 2002; Emma, born July 20, 1946. The date jumped off the paper and slammed into the center of my chest with a thud: Lily's death, May 24, 1955. I was born on May 24, 1955!

A gasp escaped my mouth; my hand went to my heart as I felt the palpitations start. I could barely speak as I told Emma, "Lily died on the day I was born." Now it was Emma's turn to appear stunned. It was her turn to feel the awkwardness of this whole fantastic set of circumstances. Just then, as Emma looked at me, I knew what it was about her look that was gnawing at me. It wasn't the fact of it being a particular kind of look, it was her eye, her right eye.

I hurriedly picked up the photo of Lily and Emma again. Yes, there it was. The same eye, the same spot on both Lily and Emma. On the outside edge of the iris was a quarter moon shape of milky white. Only I would have noticed something like that, even though it took forever to sink in. I have the same quarter moon shape of milky white on the edge of my iris, on my right eye. I don't know how common this is, all I know is Lily, Emily, Emma and I have the same characteristic mark. I asked Emma if Amber had the same mark on her right eye and she replied knowingly, "Yes, she did."

I removed my glasses and looked sideways so Emma could see my eye. I leaned in closer and said, "Explain this to me."

Emma gasped as I had just done. "Ooohh, you have the same mark of the moon on your eye, oh my— "

Finally Emma had to admit to being freaked out by the creepiness of all this. What was happening wasn't possible in any sense of the word "possible." It might have been a page from *Ripley's Believe It Or Not*, but the page had been torn out and carelessly tossed into my life.

In considering character traits I think of my own great grandmother. She had one crooked little finger. Both of my pinkies are crooked, my firstborn son has them and his son and daughter have them. No one has ever been able to determine if my mother or grandmother had crooked pinkies but it's definitely a character trait passed along by genetics. I came by my crooked fingers honestly and I like the novelty of it. Now, for some unexplained reason, I find out I have another character trait that's been passed down through the years, but this trait is in someone else's family. There is no logical explanation for how our genes were combined, but it seems they were.

As Emma and I sat and stared at each other with the photos and documents spread on the table between us, we came to the same conclusion. Something strange and unexplainable had happened back in time, maybe at the precise moment between life and death when one door closes and another opens. Somewhere on the edge of the thin line something went awry and now in 2003, we two people were brought together to decipher something we could not explain in a million years.

Somewhere within my mind I knew smidgens and portions of two people's lives from over a hundred years ago. I had put those morsels and fractions into poetry and the person who would come to read this poetry was a direct descendent of the people within my words. None of this could be explained with any reasonable level of rationality. With Emma's information fresh in my mind I went home to contemplate and dream of John Horn and Lily, the woman he loved in life and death.

# MOONWATER'S STORY

John Horn didn't grow up wanting to be a lumberjack. His teen years were filled with hatred in his heart and a blind determination to find the white man who had raped his mother, leaving her with a "bastard." He became a man knowing his mother, a full-blood Chippewa Indian, regretted the day her pregnancy came to term and hated the sight of the child who was a direct result of a drunken abusive white man. He spent his boyhood years with the love and nurturing of a woman who was not his blood mother.

The woman who gave birth to him didn't care if he lived or died. That woman vehemently wished him dead. John Horn only knew his blood mother from a faded crumpled photograph given to him by the woman who had raised him. It was the only thing left confirming with indisputable proof she was a real person. The only ancestry he could rightfully claim was his older sister, Moonwater.

Moonwater was eight years old when John Horn's mother left them alone to die. In a village along the shores of Lake Michigan, near Fort Mackinaw, there were only a few of their tribe left, most being old and feeble. Moonwater had been the daughter of a chief. During the attack by the white man the chief had been struck down, a shot fired into his chest. The chief's wife was viciously raped and left for dead while

Moonwater hid in the woods. By the time she was found the man was long gone and her mother lay unconscious, brutally beaten. Lack of cooperation from authorities resulted in no proof of the man or his whereabouts.

Throughout the long summer of 1873 her belly was swollen with a child she knew she would never love or want. When her time finally arrived and she delivered a bastard son, she waited for the raging battle within her to make a decision and then walked away, not looking back. Moonwater cared for her baby brother for two months before anyone with any authority realized it was happening. She would walk to a nearby village, borrow milk from a farmer's goat and scavenge whatever food she could find for herself. Moonwater wasn't a thief; she always intended to repay the farmer for the goat's milk. It helped keep them both alive until a kind government official came to take the monthly census.

The official, a Mrs. Roxbury, was trying to get the Indians to move to a reservation in western Michigan. The Indians who were scattered throughout the woodlands were being taken advantage of by the whisky dealers and bad influence of the white men in the area. Mrs. Roxbury was trying to save them from those disadvantages.

Mrs. Roxbury was appalled at the condition of Moonwater and her baby brother. Moonwater's long hair had come loose from her braid and was dull, lifeless and seriously matted. Her scalp was crusted and she was infested with head lice. Her face and hands were filthy from scrounging through the woods, picking berries, digging roots, old potatoes and whatever else she could find to eat. Her black eyes were sunken in. The circles under them were darker than her skin tone. She had open sores on her arms and legs from being scratched by tree branches and berry bushes. She was pathetically thin, nothing but skin and bones.

The baby was not nearly as filthy as Moonwater. He was thin but not to the extent of having his bones showing prominently. He was wrapped in a torn and dirty blanket. He had no clothing, just the blanket. Mrs. Roxbury could clearly see Moonwater was trying her best to keep him clean and fed. She feared for his health when she realized he had a seriously high fever. His face was flushed and beads of sweat were on his forehead. He had fever blisters on his upper lip. She didn't know how he continued breathing when the hacking cough gripped his tiny chest.

Her heart went out to the tiny wisp of a girl. She had met Moonwater and her mother the previous year and knew the little girl to be very articulate and smart for her age. She knelt down to Moonwater's level, asking the girl, "Where is your mother?"

Holding back tears through the choking pain of her throbbing Adam's apple she whispered, "She left us."

"How long has it been, Moonwater?"

"Two days after my brother was born, sixty-three days."

"I'd like to help you, Moonwater, will you let me do that?"

"Is my brother going to die, Mrs. Roxbury?"

"I'm going to do everything I can to make sure he doesn't."

As relief showed on Moonwater's face she said, "Then you can help us."

Mrs. Roxbury took the children home with her and bathed them, vigorously scrubbing through the layers of dirt until their skin glowed and felt like velvet. She gave the baby boy a warm bottle of milk and tucked him into a bureau drawer she lined with a feather pillow. It would have to do. The town doctor would be coming as soon as he could get there. She went to work on Moonwater's hair and after an hour of untangling and cutting out mats she did it up in two long braids. She added some leather beads she had purchased from one of the older Indian women in the village. She found a dress her own daughter had worn and altered it to fit Moonwater. She was such a tiny thing but with a little tucking and sewing the dress fit her perfectly.

Moonwater didn't say anything through the whole process and only spoke when Mrs. Roxbury spoke to her. Mrs. Roxbury didn't want to push the girl or intimidate her in any way but she needed to find out if she knew where her mother was. She feared the woman had taken her own life. Moonwater had told her the baby didn't have a name. She had been calling him John, after John the "Batiste" she had heard about from the missionaries traveling through before her mother had left. At least she thought that was his name. "He put a man named Jesus under water," Moonwater said.

Her mother's eyes would flash with hatred whenever Moonwater spoke of the missionaries. They were white men and she knew she shouldn't trust them, but Moonwater liked the stories they told and would sneak off to listen to them when her mother was asleep, or when she went to the far away place inside her mind. She had learned most of her English from the traveling missionaries or the few local storeowners who were more accepting of the village Indians.

Moonwater cautiously told Mrs. Roxbury about the night the white men came through the woods and entered the small community of Indians. They entered the birch bark lodge she lived in with her mother Star Gazer, and her father Chief Shawdawgun. There were three of them and they carried sacks full of whisky bottles. They wanted to trade for beads and moccasins. Her father refused; he wanted nothing to do with the evil water of the white man.

Moonwater was supposed to be asleep in her corner of the lodge. She quietly peeked out from under her woven blanket. She was so afraid, especially when the voices of the men became gnarled and venomous. She could smell the strong odor of the evil water they called whisky. The smell was so strong she could taste its bitterness in the back of her throat. It was mixed with the raunchy sweat and sour body odor of the men. Their eyes were shiny like glass and one man's eyes kept darting back and forth and all around the lodge. She was worried they would see her but she knew it was darker in the corner. They could not see her unless they walked to the back portion of the lodge.

One man started touching her mother's hair, standing behind her with a leer and sniffing her like a dog in heat. His teeth were yellowed and stained with tobacco. There was a gap from two missing teeth. When he spoke the slimy spittle ran through the gap, onto his bottom lip and down his bearded chin. He didn't bother to wipe it off.

His words were slurred but Moonwater could hear some words clearly enough to know they were the bad words used by the white man. He kept calling her mother a "thlut" and an "Indian whore." She had heard these words before when she went into the big town with her

44

father. They would have to walk by the saloon and the raucous words would drift out from inside where the white men would be drinking, smoking and playing a card game with money.

Moonwater noticed he was missing two fingers on his left hand. They were cut off below the second bone. The two stubs were repulsive. They were black, shriveled and dead. She couldn't take her eyes off them, expecting them to fall away from his filthy hand and drop into the dirt where they had originated.

Moonwater's father stood up, filling the lodge with his great height. His eyes were flaming orbs searing the white men with contempt. Two of the men looked at each other, one saying, "We don't want no trouble."

As they were turning to leave, the man who was still standing behind her mother grabbed her by the throat, pulled a short-barreled gun from his pocket and fired a shot into her father's chest. Chaos broke out in the lodge. The two men ran out the door, smoke from the gun filled the lodge and her father fell in a heap on the floor, his knees buckled and his legs lay grotesquely twisted beneath him. Her mother's terrifying and anguished scream filled her head as Moonwater looked at the rivulet of blood flowing from the corner of her father's mouth.

His eyes were staring at her, beginning to glass over and roll into his head. Moonwater's eyes were bulged with terror as hot tears welled, finally falling with an uncontrolled crescendo. She was frozen with fear. Her father opened his mouth to speak to her but was choking on his own blood. She heard his gurgled plea and understood, "Run."

Moonwater knew the white man had not seen her yet. She knew she had to make her body obey the command from her father, his final word. She knew she must escape before the white man discovered her and did to her what he was doing to her mother. Before she ran she took one last look at the face she knew she would never forget. As the white man ripped her mother's dress from her body, slapping and beating her into submission, Moonwater made her way out a back escape and ran into the woods to hide. She curled up under a large tree root, covered herself with leaves and bit her lip so she would have the strength to keep the contents of her stomach. She could taste the mixture of blood and salty tears as she uncontrollably trembled with terror.

First snow had not fallen yet but the nights were cold enough to see her breath in the crisp air. Sparkles appeared on the branches when the light of the moon captured their movement. Moonwater was determined to survive the cold night and she let her mind take her to a place where the eagles soar. She knew how to control her breathing and let her mind go blank so the bad pictures would fade away. She slowly fell into a deep sleep where night images were not allowed to trespass.

# STAR GAZER'S WORLD

She didn't know if her mother was dead or alive until she heard her name being called the next day, late in the afternoon. It was the voice of the old woman who occupied the lodge nearest to the one Moonwater lived in. She came out from under the leaves that had kept her warm and summoned the strength she knew was inside her. She would not cry, even if the old woman told her that her mother was dead too. She knew her father could not have survived the gunshot and she had prayed for the release of his spirit the night before.

Moonwater's story unfolded and as her voice compressed to a barely audible whisper she said, "The eyes in my mind remember his face. He did bad things to my mother. She wanted baby John to die. She couldn't come back from that faraway place. I don't know where she is, Mrs. Roxbury."

Mrs. Roxbury could not believe the fortitude of this tiny child. She knew her inner strength had to come from a source she did not understand. She had heard about the rape and beating of Star Gazer right after it happened. She had visited her back then and sent a young girl to help nurse her back to health. Star Gazer's face was so swollen from the beating she was barely recognizable. Her eyes were swollen shut for nearly two weeks, and then she was only able to see through tiny slits. It was at least a month before she was able to open her eyes fully. Her lips had been split open from repeatedly being punched with the iron fist of a man who showed no mercy toward her. They remained swollen and crusted with blood, making it nearly impossible for her to even swallow water or broth. Her upper body was cut and bruised. His filthy fingernails had scratched and gouged pieces of her skin, creating infected open sores. The insides of her thighs were bruised and her female parts and rectum were ripped and bleeding. The brute who had attacked her was a callous and sadistic animal.

Mrs. Roxbury knew that Star Gazer would never be the same. She had let her mind travel to a place where her spirit was kept comatose. She went through the everyday routine of her life but was always in an untouchable world of her own. She had made several attempts at ending her own life and expelling the bad seed growing inside her. She had eaten some poisonous berries, only to vomit the toxic substance from her stomach and suffer nothing more than a bad headache. She threw herself off a ledge along the lakeshore only to be tangled up in a tree branch, preventing her from being smashed on the rocks.

Mrs. Roxbury also recalled how the local authorities had gone through the feeble motions of conducting an investigation into the identity of the attacker and where he had run. Even then there was talk of his being a well-known trader named Zeb who had ties to the officials who were doing there damndest to force the Indians out of the area. They wanted the land, knowing there was big money in the timber industry. They had only made a few inquiries in the Indian village. None of the old people had seen or heard anything and Star Gazer was not talking—she was barely living. No one knew Moonwater had seen the white man, until now, but Mrs. Roxbury knew it was too late to do anything about it. Fearing for Moonwater's safety, she knew she could never say anything to anyone.

Eventually Star Gazer had given up trying to kill herself. Her body became swollen with a child who kicked as hard as her hatred boiled. With each passing day she was more out of touch with reality and even more so with Moonwater. The little girl was often seen bringing flowers and small treasures to place in her mother's hand. She found smooth and shiny rocks along the beach. Occasionally she would find a treasure when she walked to the big town. Once she had found a black button that turned purple when she held it up to the sun. It didn't matter how valuable she thought the treasure was, the expression on her mother's face never changed, not once. She looked through Moonwater as if she were looking into the misty steam that formed on the surface of the water on a cold day, trying only to see what was on the far side.

Star Gazer would often sit like a stone and stare off into nothing. She was sitting too close to the fire pit one day when a spark erupted from the end of a log, spitting a chip of charred wood up into the air and onto her leg. She did not move, did not even flinch. Moonwater was nearby and suddenly smelled the sickening sweetness of burning human flesh. She could hear the hissing and popping of the fire but beyond that there was the sizzling of frying meat. She turned to look at her mother and to her horror saw the hot wood chip smoking, stuck to her leg as it slowly burned a hole through her flesh, eating its way to the bone.

With the precision of a cat striking its prey she leapt up, grabbed a vessel of water and doused the fire as it was literally cooking her mother's leg. She made a salve from mud, roots and berries the way Star Gazer had shown her when she was still a tiny girl. She cleaned the burn, applied the salve and covered it with a leaf from the maple tree. It took time to heal with daily cleansing and re-application of the healing mixture, but soon the hole in her mother's leg sealed itself to a deep gouge with a jagged leathery scar.

It wasn't long afterwards when Moonwater saw her mother walk off into the woods. She was carrying a woven blanket and Moonwater knew her time to drop the baby had come. (She had been close by when her aunt had dropped her baby. The young girl had let out an agonizing scream, leaving Moonwater thinking she was surely dead. A short time later she heard the wails of her newborn cousin.) Moonwater waited in silence for her mother's scream, but that never came. She never heard the wails of any baby either. Her thoughts began to splash wildly inside her head as she envisioned her mother's dead body with a dead baby only halfway delivered, or worse.

Just as Moonwater was about to run into the woods, a forbidden thing to do, she saw Star Gazer slowly walking toward her carrying a tiny bundle. She could see the slightest movement and a wild fist waving its first greeting. Star Gazer walked up to Moonwater and silently placed her baby brother in her arms. As Star Gazer walked into the lodge Moonwater knew she was going to be fully responsible for keeping her brother alive. She knew her mother would never lay a hand or her eyes on this baby again.

Two days later, Moonwater was awakened by her baby brother's howls to be fed. As she wiped the crystals of sleep from her eyes she noticed the corner of the lodge where Star Gazer slept. Her bundle of bedding was neatly folded but it was not on the cot where it normally was. Instead, the bundle rested on the dirt floor under the makeshift cot. It was a subtle and final farewell, a sign that she would no longer need it. Star Gazer was gone and Moonwater knew she was gone in more ways than one. She knew her mother would find peace; her spirit would finally rest. She had heard stories of ancestors who had taken their own lives by walking into the ominous icy waters of Gitchegummie, the lake the white man called the Superior. It was known for never giving up its dead. Now, sixty-three days later, she was unraveling her story to Mrs. Roxbury.

# LIFE WITH MRS. ROXBURY

Over the next several years, Mrs. Roxbury did the best she could with Moonwater and John. They did well, grew fast and were very healthy. Moonwater was such a smart girl and Mrs. Roxbury was proud of the way she had adjusted in the local school. She was very well liked by the teacher and her classmates, even through she was different from all of them. The children did not show contempt for the Indians the way their parents did. The teacher taught them to respect each other.

Mrs. Roxbury was a widow. Her husband had died the year before from pneumonia and her daughter had just recently moved to Illinois to teach school. Therefore, Mrs. Roxbury could devote her time to the two children she had decided to care for. She still had her job as a government census taker but she was only expected in the office one day per week. The rest of the time was spent going from one Indian village to another to document numbers, and she could take the children with her. They looked forward to seeing their relatives and they had all accepted the fact that the children would be better off with her. The Indians were highly susceptible to diseases such as measles and smallpox. The numbers changed from week to week due to deaths, and some of the men were leaving to find work offered by the white men in the fishing trade.

In the spring of 1878 while documenting names in the Indian village along Lake Michigan she learned of an outbreak of measles and scarlet fever among the people. They were performing burial rituals nearly every day, marking the mounds with wooden markers. Some had Indian names whittled into them, others had symbols of the names. Mrs. Roxbury found one raised structure with the mark of a star with a stick figure holding up her hand, shielding her eyes and gazing into the heavens. She knew instantly she had found the grave marker for Star Gazer. It could be no one else. This shattered wife of a great chief was laid to rest with the grandeur of a highly respected woman. Her spirit joined with Chief Shawdawgun for their final reunion. She made a note in her documents but did not tell Moonwater, who was now thirteen years, and John, who was five.

Soon after, Mrs. Roxbury decided to send Moonwater to a girl's school in Pennsylvania. She knew Moonwater would have no problems adjusting. She was a very intelligent girl and Mrs. Roxbury saw no reason why she should not acquire an excellent education. Moonwater was very independent and determined to make a good life for herself, without having to rely on a rich husband someday. She had adapted well over the last few years and Mrs. Roxbury had no doubt she would become accustomed at a school away from home.

It was not common for an Indian girl to be educated at the school but they would not refuse the money. Moonwater was like a sponge when it came to reading and she too loved the idea of having the chance to be educated in all the subjects the school offered—English, arithmetic, grammar, geography and history. Mrs. Roxbury's husband had been very wealthy. He had left her with a great deal of money and it would not be a problem for her to pay the fee.

With the decision made they traveled east by train. Moonwater, who they had registered as May Roxbury at the school, would need a few new dresses, personal toiletries and shoes. They would stop off at a dressmaker and purchase skirts of percaline and crinoline, some percale housedresses and perhaps a satinette newmarket with caped shoulders. Moonwater would attend the highly respected girl's school for the next four years. She would hope to graduate with honorable grades and many awards and accreditations. She would mature into a young woman who was capable of achieving much.

During the years Moonwater attended the school in Pennsylvania, John's personality manifested itself with the headstrong stubbornness of a mule. He had never been separated from his sister and he sought attention in negative ways. He also attended school, where he was sometimes referred to as "half-breed" and was often punished for fighting and causing many disruptions in the classroom. One day he picked up a skunk by the tail, carried it into the classroom and threw it down in the middle of the room. The skunk, frightened and disoriented, started running around in circles, sending the boys and girls scattering out the door screaming at the top of their lungs, afraid they'd be sprayed with the pungent perfume of the polecat. John stood in the classroom howling with laughter. He had tied one of the skunk's back legs up, knowing it could not spray without the pumping pressure of both legs on the floor.

The fights were almost daily and went on for the years John attended the local school, but what no one seemed to notice was that the fighting was almost always triggered when one of the boys would tease, hit or say nasty things to one of the girls. No one noticed John was only defending the girls' honor. No one noticed except for the preacher's daughter, Lily. Lily thought John Roxbury—he was registered under his surrogate mother's surname for school—was the most kindhearted boy she knew, even if he did hide it under that thick hide of his.

John thought Lily was the most beautiful thing he'd ever seen. Her eyes were as blue as the waters of Lake Michigan, her hair as yellow as the peaches and cream corn the farmers were growing. She wore it long and it would sway on her back, moving like long grass in the warm breeze of a hot lazy summer day. It hung down the middle of her back almost to her waistline. The boys would often tug at it, dip it in the ink bottles or throw burrs at it, teasing her and calling her the "preacher's girl." Lily would just ignore them the way her daddy had taught her but John would become enraged at their antics, and often those same boys would end up with a bloody nose or a black eye.

When John was nine, Lily moved away. Her father was going to start a church in a town called Manistique. This town was situated on the mouth of the Manistique River, known by the Chippewa Indians as "the river with the big bay." Moonwater had spoken of this town. Her father, Chief Shawdawgun, had a brother in this town, Chief Semo Ossawinamakee. John knew from his lessons at school about the Chicago Lumbering Company cutting great virgin white pines in the surrounding areas and then sending the logs downriver to be milled in Manistique. The lumber was being use to rebuild Chicago after the great fire of 1871. It was also being shipped to England and the Midwest to build homes.

John had also heard about a place near Manistique referred to as "Indian Town." It was an area west of the town where about thirty or forty families of Indians lived in the sand dunes in wooden shacks. The women made baskets and moccasins and created beadwork they sold to the town's people and the men worked for the local sawmills. He daydreamed about the excitement of the booming town and often thought he would like to go there himself someday. He had no idea how soon it would be.

# JOHN'S HERITAGE REVEALED

Mrs. Roxbury had been sick before but never as sick as the day she almost had to crawl to Doc Wingart's office. She knew the diagnosis would be bad; the pains in her stomach were growing increasingly severe. She was starting to bleed from her rectum and the laudanum the doctor had given her two weeks earlier was starting to wear off sooner between each dose. Her stomach would spasm with such intensity it felt like an iron clamp was on the inside of her navel being pulled inward with a sadistic twisting motion. She knew the verdict would be an updated conclusion of her life expectancy. She knew she would have to make arrangements for John and inform Moonwater's school in Pennsylvania of her imminent fate. She did not want to burden her own daughter yet.

After the examination, Doc Wingart said, "I'm sorry, Mrs. Roxbury, but the growth in your stomach is eating your insides at a faster pace than I thought. The bleeding is more severe now and the severity of your pain will increase each day. I'm afraid the intensity you will have to endure will eventually drive you mad. The laudanum will lose its strength as the pain increases. I'm sorry; there is nothing more I can do for you." With these solemn words in her head, Mrs. Roxbury walked the short distance to her home and sat down to pen a letter.

She knew the location of one relative of Chief Shawdawgun. Chief Semo Ossawinamakee owned and operated a horse farm on Indian Lake, in Manistique. She knew he spoke English well but would need a translator to read the letter and help him with a reply. She felt confident he would send a quick answer. She informed him who she was, where she was located and the circumstances leading up to her guardianship of Moonwater and John. She had no idea if he even knew about the death of his brother, or the rape and death of Star Gazer. She did not want to be the bearer of this bad news but she left nothing out. Lastly she explained about her illness and looming death, the short time she had to live and her desire for John to have a home with someone she considered to be his closest relative. She knew there was no blood between them but wanted him to be raised by a man who would teach him respect for his Indian heritage. John also needed a strong man to help with his personal inner battles and his outward brawling. She sent the letter off to be posted.

John came home from school and found Mrs. Roxbury resting. Her face was ashen, she was having difficulty breathing and she would occasionally grimace in pain. He knew something was desperately wrong with Mrs. Roxbury when he saw the basin where she had been spitting blood. He also saw the addition of six more bottles of laudanum and extract of Hamamelis, used for sore throat and hemorrhaging, on her bedside table. He feared for the unknown but wanted Mrs. Roxbury to be honest with him. He said, "I am strong, Mrs. Roxbury, you can tell me anything." At nearly ten years old, John indeed was a strong boy. His love for her showed in his concern for her.

"Please, Mrs. Roxbury—tell me what is wrong with you."

Mrs. Roxbury decided then and there to be totally honest with John, about everything. "I'm very sick, John; I'm going to die soon."

John could not believe the words he had just heard from her mouth. The woman who had raised him to this point, the woman who had loved and guided him to this point, was now going to leave him. He wanted to run away, run into the woods and yell his agony into the treetops. He wanted to punch every tree in the forest. He wanted to shake Doc Wingart into changing his verdict on this dear woman's life. He wanted to, but he did none of those things.

For the next couple of hours John sat, stoically listening as Mrs. Roxbury told him the story surrounding his life, from the beginning. She told him about the man who killed Chief Shawdawgun, and the beating and violation of Star Gazer, his real mother. She told him about finding him and Moonwater after Star Gazer had deserted them, about taking them in and caring for them, raising them as if they were hers. She told him about finding the grave marker for his mother. She told him about Chief Ossawinamakee, his would-be uncle. She explained to him about her letter to him, requesting that he take over the responsibility of raising John when she died. She explained to him that it would be very soon, within a few weeks, perhaps only a few days.

John listened intently, not speaking a word. He was stunned by what Mrs. Roxbury had told him about his life. He was just a young boy but understood the seriousness of her illness. He understood the abuse of his mother by the white man; he felt the pain and suffering she must have endured. He respected Mrs. Roxbury for taking Moonwater and himself in, raising and loving them. He felt sadness when he heard about the death of Star Gazer, but at the same time, he felt such vehement hatred for her for deserting Moonwater and leaving them to a possible death. More than anything his loathing for the white man manifested itself in the form of a dead carcass with festering open sores, with maggots devouring the decaying meat.

In a few moments of vast time, John went from a carefree prankish boy to a young lad with the grownup heart of a hardened man. Tears of contempt burned the back of his eyelids. His tear ducts ached for the release of the hot molten liquid to cleanse the spirit that had just been pierced with a blunt arrow. He proudly stood, daring his tears to challenge him with their presence.

Looking into the loving eyes of the woman he held dear, with great respect he said, "Thank you, Mrs. Roxbury, thank you for being honest with me."

"John," she said, her voice lowering to a whisper, "there is something I want you to have."

"Yes, Mrs. Roxbury, what is it?"

From her pocket she took a faded photograph she had taken from her government files. She didn't think of it as stealing; she knew the files would eventually be destroyed when the Indians were moved to the reservations. She herself had been present when the photograph was taken. It had been taken a week before the vicious attack of Star Gazer. In the picture, she had the look of contentment on her face and her eyes had that special spark, which was lost after the rape.

"This is your mother, John, this is Star Gazer."

John warily took the photograph from Mrs. Roxbury and for the first time he lay eyes on the woman who had brought him into the world. His first reaction was how much Moonwater looked like her. Her hair in long black braids framed a face with high cheekbones and a proud nose. Her deep-set black eyes seemed to smolder with the red-hot coals of a fire. Her face showed the warmth of a truly fulfilled woman. John could not ignore the tug on his heartstrings. He quickly turned away a bit so Mrs. Roxbury would not notice the tear sliding down his nose.

He looked back into Mrs. Roxbury's eyes and said, "Thank you, ma'am."

With that, he slowly turned and walked outside with head held high to inhale the fresh crisp air of early autumn and contemplate his future.

•

# GRIEF STRICKEN

Within two weeks, Mrs. Roxbury had succumbed to the disease that gnawed away at her insides like a locust devouring the leaves on a tree, stripping it of all life until it ceased to look like a tree at all, but a defeated skeleton of sticks. Mrs. Roxbury barely weighed 95 pounds when she was laid to rest in a pine box and lowered into the ground. Many of the local people attended the services, remembering Mrs. Roxbury fondly. She was well known for her acts of kindness and her dedication to the Indians. Her efforts had made the Indians lifestyle a little easier to endure. She had given herself in so many unselfish ways. She would also be dearly missed by the government offices responsible for the census taking.

May (Moonwater) came from the east to attend the services of the woman who had been the staunch motherly figure in her life for the past ten years. She would miss her terribly and her grief weighed heavily on her. The emptiness she experienced left her with a feeling of having her heart torn away from her body while it stayed attached to her soul, a forlorn feeling of being lost in a wilderness too immense to do anything but wander aimlessly in circles.

She knew she had to be strong for John and she was fully prepared to quit her schooling and renew her duties in caring for him. John was trying to be so brave, so manlike. He stood tall and proud, not once letting his feelings show. Moonwater knew he would go off by himself and grieve in his own way, the Indian way. Even though he was not a pureblooded Chippewa, his ancestry flowed proudly through his veins. If he had been born under other circumstances he would have been a brave warrior; Moonwater had no doubts about that.

There was also another young woman whose grief far outweighed that of Moonwater. Mrs. Roxbury's daughter, Ellen, came from Illinois to pay her last respects to her mother and take care of her affairs. She had corresponded with her mother three weeks prior to her death. Mrs. Roxbury never let on how sick she was. She did not want to burden her daughter with the duty of performing undignified aid to her. A neighbor woman and longtime friend of Mrs. Roxbury had come in twice a day to feed her, bathe her and make sure she was getting her medicine and resting comfortably. She respected Mrs. Roxbury's wishes to not contact her daughter until the very end.

By the time Ellen received the message to come to her mother's deathbed, took the train to Mackinaw City and walked the mile to her home, it was too late to say goodbye. Her mother had passed quietly into a deep sleep. She was met by her angel to begin her journey to the other side of life, wherever that might be.

Ellen could barely stand the guilt she felt for not being with her mother in the last days of her life. She also understood the pride her mother had in life and wanted to carry with her into her death. She was relieved to know she did not suffer in her final days. She eased into a drug-induced sleep where pain was kept in abeyance, and not allowed over the threshold.

Ellen was also glad to finally meet Moonwater and John. Her mother had spoken with such compassion, pride and love toward them. Each letter she received had some news to relate about their progress over the years. She felt an affinity to them that became stronger knowing they were the only relations she had left, aside from the fact they were not blood relations. She knew they would all grieve for a long time over their mother and mentor.

Mrs. Roxbury's attorney came to the house after the service and told

Ellen she would need to come to his office to take care of the details of Mrs. Roxbury's affairs. She was intelligent enough to understand her mother had probably provided for all three of them, and knowing how meticulous she was with her work, would probably have every detail taken care of. She could be strong and do what had to be done and then she would leave for Illinois. Her life was there, even more so now.

# THREE SEPARATE JOURNEYS

Mrs. Roxbury had indeed provided for the children, right down to the details of which of her personal possessions each one would receive and a great deal of money which was set up in a trust fund for each of them. Their was money to provide the school with May's tuition, money donated to the school where Ellen taught, and money for John's future education.

During the three weeks it took of the three of them to pack their belongings, they grew closer and felt more like a family. There was a special bond between them and Mrs. Roxbury would go on living in each of them. A letter came from Chief Ossawinamakee, agreeing to have John come to live with him. Ellen would return to her teaching job in Illinois. May decided she would return to Pennsylvania to finish out her last school year.

A week before they were to leave, a family bought the house their mother had left them. As indicated in her last wishes, the money from the sale of her home went into a fund to educate the Indian children in the area. Ellen, May and John had more then enough money for their needs, they would not miss what money the sale of the home had brought. Mrs. Roxbury had a heart of gold when it came to the Indian children she had come in contact with over the years. She wanted to do something good for them.

In late September of 1883 the family said their good-byes. Ellen would return to Illinois by way of a schooner. May would take the next train heading east to Pennsylvania, and John was going by way of the schooner *North Star,* heading west on Lake Michigan to Manistique. They all promised to stay in close contact until they could be together again. Circumstances would not warrant the three of them ever being together again.

Two schooners docked in Manistique that day. One carried, among other passengers, three brothers who had come from Germany by boat, then by train to Hermansville, footpath to Escanaba and on to Manistique by schooner. In addition, on the boat were masons and carpenters who would build the Catholic church that year. John overheard one of the men referring to one of the others as "Sebastian." He had never heard such a name and thought it sounded honorable and stoic. He repeated the name over and over and it stuck in his head like the tune of a church hymn.

John's schooner had docked at the harbor and he was met by Chief Ossawinamakee, his new mentor. He was a majestic looking figure against the dawning red sky of late autumn. He stood tall and stone-faced, his chiseled silhouette accenting his prominent nose. He had a blanket wrapped around his shoulders for warmth and protection against the wind. He greeted John, helped him up onto a gallant palomino and they rode off toward the farm that would be John's new home.

May's train arrived in Pennsylvania within a few minutes of its estimated time. There had been no problems and she enjoyed the trip with its views of the forest and lakes along the way. The natural world she saw always made her think about her Indian heritage, and the many stories she had heard as a child about the spirits of the ancestors being within the animals of the forest. She always felt close to nature and she enjoyed traveling by train and seeing so much of it.

Ellen did not fair so well. The schooner she was on hit a reef near the shoreline when they tried to take refuge in a storm. The captain, crew and all the passengers perished in the chaotic waters of Lake Michigan. Ellen was knocked unconscious by a mast that fell after snapping in the strong gales. At least she was spared the tortuous death by drowning the other passengers had suffered. Many of the bodies were recovered the next day when they washed ashore near one of the larger towns along the lakeshore.

May and John would never hear from Ellen again, and would never know what had happened to the woman they considered their sister. In the late 1800s it was not always easy for news to travel from one area to another. The passenger list had been destroyed when the schooner went down, so some of the passengers were never identified. May and John thought Ellen had forsaken them. Maybe she had decided she would just go on with her life and not think about the past, or them. They hated the thought, but they had no other alternative when they received no word from her.

# JOHN AND SEMO

Chief Ossawinamakee had been deeded property near Indian Lake in Manistique in one of the many treaties that were in effect. He was also given the ownership of over 200 draft horses. These horses were raised for use in the logging industry. Logs were cut in the winter months and hauled on massive wooden sleds pulled by these draft horses. It was easier to haul the tremendous logs over the snow where they would await the spring thaws, eventually being put afloat in the Manistique River to arrive at the sawmills.

John worked alongside his Uncle Semo day after day, learning the intricacies of raising these much sought after workhorses. He missed Moonwater terribly and would receive at least one letter each month with the news she shared from out east. She talked about joining him when her schooling was complete. She hoped to open a business in Manistique. Using the money left her by Mrs. Roxbury, she could invest in a fairly good-sized saloon or boarding house. She was business minded and knew there was money to be made.

John thought about Lily in those days; he knew she and her preacher father had moved to Manistique the previous year. He only went into town every other month for supplies, usually riding in the back of the wagon with his uncle driving the team of horses. He always hoped to run into her someday while they were in town taking care of their business. He really had no idea which church her father had built, there were so many of them now. He never had the time to look for her and he was a little embarrassed to ask his uncle for fear of being ridiculed for his infatuation with a girl.

He would close his eyes and visualize her warm blue eyes and the smile that would light up her whole face, creating a twinkle in those eyes of hers. He wasn't one to sit around and get google-faced about a girl, but it would have been wonderful to set eyes on her again, maybe just to talk about familiar things from their days in Mackinaw City. Then, just as quickly, a rabbit would run across the path of the horses causing a fracas and his thoughts would be jolted into reality. They would finally arrive in town, take care of their errands and return to the farm and their everyday routine duties. Lily would sit in silence in the back of his mind, time would pass and she would surface again into his daydreams.

One day John was in a wooded area on the back part of the property. He was following a well-beaten path leading to a creek where the horses strayed once in awhile. The horses were often found standing in the creek, cooling themselves. He was looking for a pony that had gone missing from the herd. His mind was wandering to a particular day over a year ago when Lily ran up to him in the schoolyard. She was out of breath, the hem of her dress was torn and her face had a scratch covered with a streak of mud mingled with her tears. Two boys were chasing her with a dead snake. One was twirling it around over his head and flinging it through the air into her path—

Suddenly his thoughts were interrupted when, from out of nowhere, an enraged bull came out of the woods, running with a deranged fierceness directly into his path. The bull stopped dead in its tracks when it saw John. It started pawing the ground, intent on the kill. The bull had a look in its eyes of disoriented madness as it started to charge John. With the quick instinct only an Indian has, John grabbed the bull by one horn before it could force its weapon into his vulnerable stomach. John had visions of his guts being literally ripped from him and tossed on the ground like stuffing from a rag doll. He threw his body aside while still hanging onto the horn, his feet leaving the ground in his attempt to jump out of the way. The bull's head reared back, throwing John into the air. His body smashed against a tree and slid to the ground. In a dazed state he could see the enormous animal turn towards him, begin to paw the ground and throw his head down for the climactic final kill. John knew he was going to die. He closed his eyes and prepared for the release of his spirit.

Simultaneously he heard a whistling ping and a load crack echoing against the trees. Hearing the grunt and whistling snort of the bull he opened his eyes to see the bull stopped in its tracks, head down and blood blowing out its nose with each struggling breath. Its eyes were burning with contempt, enraged at the finality of its attempt at goring its victim. The bull's knees began to buckle, its legs began to stumble and it collapsed from its own dead weight. It finally crashed to the ground and gave a great heaving release of its final breath.

John was never more relieved to see the enormous shape of his inconspicuous Uncle Semo, holding a smoking muzzleloader rifle. He made his way toward John and, picking him up from the ground, he said, "It's a good day for that bull to die." By the time John regained his wits, Uncle Semo was making his way down the path, rifle slung over his shoulder.

From that day, John would be known as John Bull Horn. Chief Ossawinamakee knew he deserved to be given an Indian name after the harrowing experience. He had witnessed the courage and strength of a boy grabbing a bull's horn in an attempt to save his own life. He was worthy of the name and it would later be shortened to just John Horn.

It wasn't long before nearly everyone in Manistique, with the exception of Lily, had heard the story about John Horn. He was considered one of the bravest ten-year-old boys anyone had ever heard of. The story flew through the saloons and carried to the many logging camps, as a small boy became the legendary hero of men considered to be meaner than snot and tougher than dirt. The cooks and shanty boys would repeat the story during every meal. They never tired of telling it and the lumberjacks never tired of hearing it told. The lumberjacks would talk about John Horn for many years and each time the story was told someone added their own rendition of the day "the boy killed the bull with his own bare hands." Those who knew the real story would just chuckle and agree.

After a year of living with Chief Ossawinamakee, not attending school but learning the ropes of the horse breeding and trading business, it was decided John would be sent to a school at Red Rocks Bluff, north of Manistique near the town of Marquette, to further his education. A missionary, Bishop Baraga, had traveled through and set up missions and schools to educate the Indians in the area. John was eleven now and Chief Ossawinamakee felt it would be best for his future. So off he went, to be schooled for the next three years.

# PREACHER TOM AND LILY

When Preacher Thomas Abrams and his daughter Lily arrived in Manistique the year before, they were met at the dock by an old Indian, Chief Ossawinamakee. It was tradition for him to meet as many of the incoming schooners as he could. He loved sitting near the docks and watching the great masts appear on the horizon in all their glory and make their way majestically into the harbor of Manistique. He greeted each and every passenger, at least those who would acknowledge him. Some people still balked when it came to the Indians in the area. No reason—they were just set in their ways.

Lily was in awe of the tall stout figure awaiting their arrival. His presence seemed to demand great respect. His piercing black eyes looked at her with the warmth of a blazing hearth. Bending on one knee, down to her level of vision, he took her tiny hand in his massive one and said, "Welcome to Manistique." The difference in their tone of skin made a striking picture. His skin, darkened by his bloodline and constant exposure to the sun and weather-beaten by the elements, appeared even more dark in contrast to the fairness of Lily.

As Lily timidly smiled back at this giant of a man, the chief caught the faint sparkle in her eyes. He also couldn't help but notice the milky white spot on her eye, shaped like a quarter moon. He was intrigued by this unexpected reminder of his long-dead grandmother. His grandmother had been the best storyteller there was back in the old days. She had spoken of these special marks on the eyes of the Indians who were believed to be very gifted in the ways of the ancestors. He had yet to see the mark on any Indian, and now he was looking into the eyes of a delicate little blonde-haired girl who had the special slice of the moon on her eye. The whispering spirits were speaking to him. He didn't understand it but he didn't question it either. The chief stood and offered his hand to the man whom he assumed was the new preacher who was expected to arrive.

"Welcome to Manistique, I am Chief Ossawinamakee, Semo."

"Thomas Abrams, folks call me Preacher Tom, and this is my daughter Lily." He wondered at the articulation of this seemingly intelligent chief.

Semo bent again and, looking at Lily's mysterious eyes, said, "You'll like it here in Manistique, Lily. You are indeed as beautiful as a lily, but I will call you 'girl with moon eye,' if it's all right with you."

Lily, giggling at her funny new name, said, "Thank you, sir, I think I will like it here too."

It took Lily about three months to adjust to living in a strange and new town, but once she was settled in, she loved living in Manistique. Her father had built a small church on the outskirts of town and had a decent number of people who came to worship with them. Most of the people never actually became members of the church. They were drifters passing through town or some of the lumberjacks who came to town once a month. Some of the lumberjacks went directly to a saloon when they were in town, others stopped by to say hello to Lily and Preacher Tom.

Preacher Tom was loved by all the people who met him. He was a little soft spoken in regular conversation but his voice could boom out from the pulpit. He never held back the truths of the Bible as he understood it, and was always open to suggestions and translations from his parishioners and acquaintances. He was well spoken and honest, never sugarcoating his words with what the people wanted to hear. He was never afraid to speak boldly and stand up for what he believed in. He was widely respected by many people.

Many of the neighboring women would bring pies or leftovers from their tables. They had learned that Preacher Tom's wife had died several years earlier and all of them took up the special task of helping to raise six-year-old Lily. She was the most enjoyable and free-spirited little girl. She always had at least twenty new questions to ask when anyone visited. Without fail she always asked about the Indian chief she had met on the docks the day of her arrival. She had only seen him the one time but she felt a spiritual connection with him, and he reminded her of her friend John, from Mackinaw City.

She often thought about all the funny crazy things he had done for attention. She also remembered all the times he had saved her from the older boys' rough teasing, the many times he had defended her honor by blackening eyes or making the school bullies retreat. She carried her fondness for John in a special nook in her heart. She wondered how he was doing in Mackinaw City with Mrs. Roxbury, and if she would ever see him again. They never heard any news from there, which placed him all the further from her. Slowly the months turned into a year and she did not realize John had moved to Manistique and was living with the same Indian chief she had met on her first day at the docks.

Their lives' paths would cross many, many times in the next few months, but they were never aware of how close they would come to bumping into each other while in town. They never knew how many times their shoes had scuffed through the same dirt on the streets, their arms had reached up into the same licorice jar at the general store or the jars of the much-loved favorite jujubes and jawbreakers. Their feet had waded through the same creek that flowed into the lake, their hands had brushed across the same white picket fence in front of the hotel in town, their legs had dangled from the same tree branch in back of the livery store. Their paths had crissed and crossed and crissed and crossed but it wasn't in the almighty plan for them to connect, not yet.

# JAKE

In finishing her fourth year of school, Moonwater had made good on her vow to finish with honorable grades. She was well educated in the sense of being able to purchase and run her own business. She had received word from her Uncle Semo in Manistique of John's departure for the school at Red Rocks Bluff. She knew he would be there for the next several years and planned to make the best of starting a business and being well established when he returned.

She journeyed again by train to Mackinaw City and then by schooner to Manistique. The journey was a long and tiring one, taking nearly a month because of storms. When she arrived at the dock in Manistique, the faithful steward of greeting was there to meet her. Smiling and waving she knew the stout figure on shore must be her Uncle Semo. He greeted her with open arms and she ran into them with a heartfelt longing to be with family once again. She was home.

She missed John terribly and planned to journey by horseback to visit with him before she would undertake her business venture. First, she would settle into the home she planned to have built with some of the money left her by Mrs. Roxbury. Her boarding house would be constructed right next door. She had done her homework and knew there was a set of brothers who were carpenters. They were honest hard-working men who put in a long day and always did meticulous work. Their reputation was unmarred and she looked forward to going over her plans with them.

Moonwater, choosing to continue using the name May, met with Sebastian, one of the brothers. He agreed to start on the building of her house the following week, and planned to be finished in about a month. They would then start construction of the boarding house, which would take at least another two months. May decided she would visit John during the construction of her home, and return by early autumn.

Accepting the loan of one of her uncle's finest horses, she began her journey to Marquette to visit with her brother. Uncle Semo sent a trusted man to travel with her. It wasn't always safe for women to travel alone and the trails lead through a forest inhabited by wolves, black bears and bobcats, just to name a few of the wild animals that could prove dangerous.

Jake, the man who guided her, was a family man, trusted by Uncle Semo and anyone else you bothered to ask. He was big and burly at over six feet with strong wide shoulders, and walked with a slight limp. Uncle Semo had told her he had been shot in the leg by a man trying to rob his neighbor of a few horses. He was a handsome man with wavy auburn hair and a beard he only let grow a few days at a time. He always ended up shaving it off. "Too picky," he'd say.

His wife was accustomed to him being gone for several weeks at a time. He often guided people through the trails to surrounding areas. He met many men who arrived almost daily at the docks and took them into the woods to various lumber camps, some as far away as Seney, which was about thirty miles from Manistique. This trip was a bit further but was a special favor to Chief Ossawinamakee and he didn't mind that it would take about a month to complete the round trip. He would do anything to help a friend.

"So, tell me Jake, how long have you lived in Manistique?" May was curious and not afraid to ask about people's lives.

Jake smiled at her. "About a year now."

"Have you worked for my uncle the entire time?"

"As a matter of fact, I have."

May and Jake became close on their trek through the woods. May told him her whole life story, even the bad parts about her mother. She felt a loyalty in him and sensed she could trust him with even the worst parts of her life. A few times he comforted her, lending his shoulder and drying her tears with his shirtsleeve. She felt silly afterwards, but it helped bolster a relationship she was sure would last a lifetime. She hadn't cried since Mrs. Roxbury's funeral and she certainly felt refreshed, her spirit renewed.

She learned that Jake and his wife had been married for ten years, and than all ten of those years they had tried without success to have a child. Jake wanted nothing more than to have a son, or even a daughter. It didn't matter as long as they could only be blessed with a child. His wife had been to many doctors, all who had come to the same conclusion: when the time was right there was no reason why she could not bear children. She was told to just be patient, God would provide her with a child when He saw fit. Jake had to admit to May that he had given up several years ago. His wife still hoped.

Early one morning, a couple of days into their journey, May awoke to the blood-curdling screaming cry of what sounded like an angry cat. Her heart pounded wildly as she sat up in her bedroll and watched Jake fire a shot over her head. With eyes as wide as pie tins she watched in horror as a huge bobcat fell from a tree branch and landed at her feet. In shocked disbelief, she opened her mouth to scream and nothing would come out from her stunned vocal cords. Jake grabbed the beast by the tail, yanking and heaving its great weight around until he had pulled it some distance away from May. Jake returned, put the coffee pot on the fire, looked at May and said, "I think he had his eye on you for breakfast, May."

She nearly fainted dead away. Jake had saved her life and she would be eternally grateful to him. All she could manage to say was a choked, "Thank you, Jake." He just smiled in his nonchalant way and handed her a hot cup of coffee. May knew she owed her life to him. Words were insufficient to express her gratitude. Their friendship was cemented with an invincible bond.

Jake became like a father to her as May came to know him more and more. He had come from a family of seven brothers, and was of Irish descent. They were raised by a strict Catholic father who taught them all to have great respect for their mother, and all women, which they did. Three of his brothers had died very young, two to the smallpox virus, one to tuberculosis. One was a sawyer at the Hall & Buell Sawmill in Manistique. His remaining two brothers were both captains on sailing vessels. One, she found out, was the captain of the schooner that had brought her to Manistique. Such a small world they lived in.

In a little over a week they arrived outside of Marquette. She knew she would be seeing her brother soon and she sang joyfully, making up words as she went. The many birds joined in with their own harmony. Jake laughed his great booming laughter as she sang so off-tune her horse's ears pricked back from the irritation. May giggled and laughed along with her newfound friend.

# PLEAS FOR HELP

Lily was running, her heart racing wildly, trying to keep pace with her dilemma. Her boots, heavy with water and muck, were sucking her down into the black silt with each desperate step she ran. Her blonde hair, flying free, was snagging on brambles and low branches, the crippled gnarled twig fingers ripping out tiny patches of her hair. Even the giant trees seemed to be a threat, closing in on her.

Chasing behind her were two local boys, more bullies. They seemed to follow her everywhere, at every stage in her life. They had caught her alone walking through the woods, picking wild flowers. She knew she was in trouble when the one boy leered at her, running his eyes over her body as if he were seeing her naked. Just as she turned to run he grabbed for the front of her dress, pulling a couple of buttons away from the fabric. She was only slightly exposed but felt so violated. If she ran fast enough, maybe the filthiness of his hand would leave her.

Lily knew her way through the woods. She had walked this way many times, enjoying the sounds of twittering birds, especially loving the one that sounded like a kitten's meow. There were other chirps and chitters from unseen scurrying creatures, letting each other know a human was invading their sanctuary. She loved walking alone in the woods, daydreaming mostly about John Roxbury.

*Oh God, where was he now when she needed to be saved, where was he with his bold fist squaring off on the bully's nose or leaving a shiner on his eye?* Those were her desperate pleading thoughts as she ran for her life, or more than likely, her virtue. Her mind was racing as fast as her legs. *Help me, John Roxbury, please help me!*

After slipping and falling several times, Lily finally broke clear of the wooded area just down the road from her father's church. The boys, out of breath and gasping for air, had given up the chase, vowing to each other, "Next time she won't get away, we'll get a feel of what's under her dress if it's the last thing we do." They made the pact with a brush of their fist on each other's chins.

These boys had peeked into the windows of many ladies in town. They knew what was under those clothes and now they wanted to touch. They wanted to touch Lily. They had had their eyes on her for a long time. That long yellow hair and eyes the color of the lake when the sun hit it just right. Not blue, not green, but a smidgen of both. Those full luscious lips of hers were begging to be kissed. Just the pureness of her excited them.

These boys were old enough to have experienced the hardness that made their pants bulge. They had watched studs, bulls and boy dogs mounting females and sticking their hard bones into someplace that made the females stand still for it. They knew what it was all about, they just had never done it yet. They wanted to "do it" with Lily.

Lily had never run so fast. She still couldn't believe she'd outrun those boys. Leaving her muddy stockings and boots by the back door she closed herself up in her room so she could clean up, mend her dress and thank God for being safe from harm. She was old enough now, nearly thirteen, to know the change that came over boys when they looked at her. The teasing had gone from throwing burrs in her hair and throwing snakes at her to leering and trying to touch her intimate private areas with their groping filthy hands. She hated boys.

If she were ever to let someone touch her in that way, it would be as the wife of John Roxbury. But where was he? She lay down on her bed and let her thoughts take her away, sailing on a soft summer breeze back to Mackinaw City when she knew he was never far away. She knew without any hint of doubt in her heart she was in love with John Roxbury, always would be, and someday they would be together again, forever.

As Lily was drifting off to sleep, John, one hundred miles away, was fighting with an overwhelming dread. His chest was tight and heavy, crushing each breath into a huff. He sensed, he knew, something wasn't right. He hated these spells he had so often. He knew something was dreadfully wrong, but not just anything—it was something with Lily. He'd had these strange things happen in the past, as far back as when he was eight years old. Once he began to recognize the sensation and not fight it he knew each time Lily needed him. He knew she had begun to need him more and more.

# MANISTIQUE

.

John had finished school in 1888 and had found work with Paul White. Now in 1890, they were building a road around Presque Isle, in Marquette. It was a good job but he wanted to be in Manistique, nearer to both Lily and Moonwater. He thought he wouldn't have any trouble finding work on the log run or at the Hall & Buell Sawmill. He knew he had to be near Lily. The desperation weighed on him, making him determined to find her and pledge his love even if she laughed in his face.

He knew he had been in love with Lily from the moment he laid eyes on her in Mackinaw City. It had been six years since he'd left Manistique; he was no longer a boy but a fine young man. He regretted not being able to take the time to find her when he had lived with Uncle Semo. He had always been so busy with the horses and he was only eleven. Could he have been a little more determined to find her back then? He asked himself that question a hundred times and he didn't like the answer. Now, he was going to do something about it.

It seemed like forever since Moonwater and Jake had visited him in school. So much had happened since then. Aside from his finishing school, he had worked with Mr. White on various projects, mostly clearing forestland, building roads and constructing buildings for new businesses in the fast growing area. He was a hard worker, a valued employee who put in long hours not caring about the severe weather conditions and backbreaking work. John was an honest man and put in an honest day's work.

Moonwater and Jake's visit now seemed like a lifetime ago. He received monthly letters from her, catching him up on all the news the way she always did. She was now the proud owner of one of the most famous boarding houses in the Upper Peninsula, Ravenwood. On the west side of town she knew it had a reputation, but it didn't seem to bother her. She had made it clear to the girls she hired that it was at their own discretion the way they chose to entertain the boarders.

Usually the men who stayed were only there for a day or two. Mostly businessmen passing through, they enjoyed the fabulous meals served in the dining room. Moonwater had hired the best chef she could find. Famous for his soups and sauces, Raoule was a Frenchman. She maintained a saloon where the men could relax and enjoy the finest whisky while playing a game of poker or just listening to the piano player and songstress. Some of the men wanted the simple enjoyment of friendly companionship, others wanted more of an intimate rendezvous. Moonwater left that decision up to the girls. What they did in the privacy of their own rooms was their own business.

Manistique, the town with the river running through it, had most of the stores, saloons, and churches located on the east side of town. The Chicago Lumbering Company owned most of the town, except an area near the river. There it was that you could count over twenty saloons, the most famous being Nessman Saloon and Heffron Saloon, both of which had gambling rooms.

The Weston Lumbering Company had moved in around 1883, operating two sawmills. There was an iron company, a lime company and a leather company as well as several hotels. One majestic hotel was not far from the dock. The Ossawinamakee Hotel dominated the main part of town, named after the faithful greeter, Uncle Semo. It stood as proud as he did and May and John were both happy for the honor bestowed on their uncle.

There were still daily schooners coming and going, bringing

immigrants into Manistique and taking lumber out. It was a little melting pot for the French Canadian, German, Finnish, Swedish and Austrian people looking for work and enjoying the excitement of a new town on the shores of Lake Michigan.

The town was booming. With three sawmills running twenty-four hours a day and several logging camps in the outlying areas, each housing 800-1000 men, the town was as busy as any small town could be. The men would come in from the camps during their off time and proceed to spend their entire month's wages on liquor and gambling or supplies. Most of the men were single and were more interested in raising hell than raising a family. John knew he was not going to be like most of those men.

John also knew where Lily was. Moonwater had located the church her father had started nearly a decade ago, years that felt like a lifetime. The church was also located on the west side, only two miles down the road from where the Ravenwood stood. He was going to knock on Preacher Tom's door and his hopes were to see Lily. He couldn't wait to set his feet in Manistique again. The town with the river running through it would soon be his home.

His uppermost thought was Lily. He did not once consider the reception he would get from a God-fearing preacher with a lovely daughter he watched like a hawk. It never occurred to John that Preacher Tom would hastily run him off when he realized he was the brother of a brothel owner. Ravenwood was nothing more than a house of harlots as far as Preacher Tom was concerned. God would dole out his judgments upon them all. No man of faith would stay within the walls of a boarding house with women draped all over the place, serving whisky as if it was water. John had no way of knowing Preacher Tom had such strong feelings about the boarding house but he would soon find out.

# Welcome Home

The summer of 1892 finally brought John to Manistique. He had finished work on the roads and projects in and around Marquette. He was reluctant to leave such a good job. Mr. White had been good to him, not only paying him well but also teaching him many important skills. He had been like a father to him and John had gained a great respect for him and his family. John thought Mr. White held out hopes of having him for a son-in-law someday.•

Mr. White's daughter was a beautiful girl with close-set scarlet eyes in an ivory face. Her black hair flowed free with natural ringlets. She was a tiny strand of a girl and would no doubt make some man a good wife, just not John. His heart belonged to Lily and no other girl would ever do his heart right. If he never had the opportunity to be with Lily he would die a lonely man. His eyes saw only her in all his day and night dreams.

John arrived on the back of a fine horse, a farewell gift from Mr. White. His long black hair flipped freely in the wind, matching the whipping movement of his horse's mane. The stallion stood sixteen hands high. He was jet black with a perfect white star right between his eyes. He was Arab and Morgan, favoring the high-strung Arabian in his bloodline. John knew he would be able to endure the long trip and be sure-footed through the winding trails running through the forest between Marquette and Manistique.

His first stop was Ravenwood. He was barely off his horse when the front door burst open and Moonwater was bouncing down the steps and jumping into his arms. John picked her up and gracefully lifted her above his head while spinning her in a joyful circle. Her giggles and shrieks could be heard inside which brought some of the customers and girls running outside to see what the commotion was. They stood on the front porch, each with their own interpretation of the scene before them.

Most of the girls were swooning over this forceful man they knew to be May's brother. They had all heard so much about him but his handsome features went far beyond what any of them had expected. As they stood and watched some of them were undressing him in their minds while others considered the new man husband material. Still others just admired the bond between brother and sister.

The men watched with mixed emotions. None of them liked competition. Most of them had their favorite girl and didn't like to share her even though they knew they did. It was easy to ignore the advances of a man just passing through, but they knew this man was sticking around for a while. To some he was a threat; they noticed the Colt-45 strategically hanging on his hip. Others welcomed the new blood for the poker games they played. Some of the betting produced large piles of cash on the tables and any addition to the games was always welcome.

Finally Moonwater's feet touched the ground. She spun around to the clapping and cheering of the crowd that had gathered on the porch of Ravenwood. "Everyone, this is my brother John!"

As they made their way into the boarding house John shook hands with several men, received kisses on the cheek from some of the women and was eventually sitting at a table with a plate of beef roast and potatoes piled high enough for two men. Moonwater sat across from him with a cup of coffee, anxious to hear about his trip home, for now indeed, he was truly home.

Outside, making their way down the dirt road were Preacher Tom and Lily. He hated having to drive by Ravenwood to get home but it only served to remind him of the hard work he had chosen to do for the Lord. There were many sinners and it was his duty to get them to repent and change their lives for the better. He never failed to try to ignore the comings and goings at Ravenwood. He did not want Lily exposed to the brashness of some of the women. At times they could be seen climbing the outside stairs, escorting men to their rooms. He could not understand why God had allowed the boarding house to be built in such close proximity to his church, but he knew God worked in mysterious ways.

They had watched the hullabaloo as they were nearing the boarding house. They heard the screams of glee and watched as the owner was spun around by a man and escorted into the front door. Just another lost soul passing through town as far as Preacher Tom was concerned.

Lily knew John's sister Moonwater owned Ravenwood and that she went by the name of May. She had run into her at the hat shop one day and was surprised to have Moonwater recognize her. "Lily—aren't you Lily Abrams?"

Lily remembered the day as if it was yesterday. She had quickly averted her eyes from the stranger who knew her name. She knew she was the owner of Ravenwood from the talk at school from the older girls. She also knew if her father caught her speaking to her he would never stop preaching to her about the harlots and whores. Lily thought her father judged too harshly but she never dared mention to him how she thought Jesus would react—after all, hadn't he been able to touch the life of Mary Magdalene?

"Lily, I'm Moonwater, don't you remember me from Mackinaw City?"

When Lily raised her eyes the first thing she saw was the similarity between Moonwater's eyes and how she remembered John's to be. With a shy smile she said, "You're John Roxbury's sister, aren't you?"

"Yes, how are you, Lily?"

"Fine, thanks."

Moonwater could tell Lily was self-conscious about speaking to her, more so about being seen with her. She knew of the reputation she had for running Ravenwood. The rumors were far worse than reality, but it was a small town with lots of religious folks and she knew she was better off just to keep to herself. "I'm sorry, Lily, I won't keep you. It was nice talking to you." She couldn't very well ask her to stop by for a visit.

Just when Lily was about to ask about John, Mrs. Clark came into the hat shop, threw a disgusted look at Moonwater, whooshed Lily out the door and stuck her nose in the air and proceeded to look at the new hats with a manner of haughtiness surrounding her.

Over a year had passed since that day at the hat shop. Mrs. Clark had miraculously never said anything to her father about seeing her that day. Lily had never seen Moonwater again when she was alone but had vowed to herself that when given the opportunity again she was going to ask her about John.

As their horse-drawn wagon passed Ravenwood now she caught a glimpse of the happiness and beauty of Moonwater's glowing face. She felt the lump form in her throat, just hurtful enough to make her eyes water and her heart plunge into a lonely ache. She didn't dare turn around for a last look at Moonwater and the stranger by her side. Her thoughts were swirling with the dust they left behind. *Where are you John Roxbury?*

# TO THE RESCUE

John stood in the darkness of the tree line watching the worshipers file out of the small white building. The faint breeze was not enough to relieve the stickiness of the sweat on his brow. His hair, tied back in a braid, felt heavy on his collar. The persistent buzzing of gnats and the almost invisible swarm of noseeum around his face made him question his lack of sense. He'd never seen anything like it; the insect population was multiplied due to the close proximity of a stagnant pond. Surrounded by a stand of cedar trees, it was a haven for breeding. He knew enough not to start swatting. It only caused the pests to swarm in a frenzy, furiously seeking the warm-blooded host body—namely, his.

John had mastered the ability to ignore the blood-sucking parasites. His mind was better occupied with keeping his eyes peeled for Lily. He was so sure he'd see her leaving the church service. He knew she would never be allowed to miss her father's sermon. He was too strict of a preacher to allow for a bad example to be set forth by his own daughter. He waited until the last person stood on the step shaking hands with Preacher Tom. He watched as the last horse and wagon made its way down the well-beaten narrow road toward town. His heart sank in his gut with the thud the way only a jilted lover's can. Where was Lily?

It had been three weeks since John had arrived at Ravenwood.

Moonwater had given him a welcoming celebration the boarders would not soon forget. The food was prepared to perfection, the money piled up on the gaming tables and the whisky flowed freely. John had never developed a taste for liquor and deep down he was grateful. He'd seen the affect it had on so many men. He had lost his friend Walter while working in Marquette. He had been hit over the head after leaving a saloon. It was bitter cold that night and the owner had found Walter the next morning, a frozen contorted shape in the snow. His skull had been broken open by the heavy beam that lay beside his body. Blood and brain matter told the story of his violent demise. The scarlet and blackness of the blood was in vivid contrast to the pure white snow. His pockets were turned inside out, the work of a murdering thief who was never found.

The saloon owner had told his account of an argument during a card game. A drifter had accused Walter of cheating and argued about his right to have the gold pocket watch Walter had worn proudly. He had a good description of the suspect who was long gone. He had long straggly graying hair, and spoke with a lisp because of the two teeth missing from his bottom layer of teeth. The rest of his teeth were badly stained from tobacco. His left hand was monstrous looking, with two blackened finger stubs.

That description told John this man was more than the murderer and thief who had taken his best friend's life. He was the same man who had killed Chief Shawdawgun. He was the animal who had savagely beaten and raped his mother. In actuality, John would not be here if not for this animal. In stark reality he was John's father by blood, his mortal enemy by instinct and his target for revenge. His day was coming as John felt the vehemence flow through his veins as surely as his tainted blood.

Moonwater had tearfully described to John only a week ago the night that had changed her life. She recounted with deep sorrow and intense emotion the night of her father's murder and the violent rape of their mother. The attacker's face was forever engraved in her memory. She too had made a vow to herself that would appease her restless psyche and avenge the hatred burning in her soul. When John heard her describe the man he was struck dumb with the bald truth that this was the same man who had killed Walter. To think he had touched his life, not once but twice, was more than he could comprehend.

Suddenly John was yanked from his reverie by the now familiar tightness in his chest. The crushing sensation took away his breath as he felt the weight descend upon him. Lily was in trouble. Clutching his chest he heard a high-pitched scream that pierced his heart with a searing stake. He jerked to attention, running toward the woman's screams for help. The fleeting thought *Don't let it be Lily* disappeared as fast as it had come, as he knew with certainness it was Lily. He raced across the road and into the stand of trees. There was a narrow pathway through overgrown underbrush leading to a secluded area beyond the church. He had found it in his wanderings. At the time he thought it might be one of Lily's favorite spots. He had felt her presence there.

He ignored the stinging strikes to his face as he dodged the back-slapping branches. The tangled menagerie of thicket came to life, grabbing at his ankles and shins in an attempt to make him fall to the ground where he might be sacrificed to the gods of the woods. John was too sure-footed to succumb to the madness of the melee. As another blood-curdling scream pierced the solitude of the woods, he broke through into the clearing. His only thought was to reach her.

In flashes he saw her fighting her attacker. All he saw were arms swinging, fists flying, legs kicking and bodice ripping as her attacker knocked her to the ground. The attacker finally straddled her, holding both her wrists above her head to subdue her. As he bent his face toward hers the terror in her scream reached a new dimension. John's heart nearly ripped in two.

As he reached for the man and grabbed the scruff of the neck his anger had reached a boiling point. John jerked his head back so violently he heard the distinct snap of a broken vertebra. The would-be rapist screamed in pain and demented fury. Being caught off guard was a disadvantage for the man. He never had a chance to fight back as John pummeled him into the dirt with iron fists. The man's face was barely recognizable as it was smeared and caked with blood and mud. John only stopped when he heard Lily whimper.

When Lily opened her eyes, for a minute she was confused, her first thoughts hazy. Her last comprehension was of feeling the weight of her attacker suddenly being lifted off her, and then she must have fainted. She tried desperately to make her eyes focus on the distorted figure coming to her rescue. Her heart leaped into her throat when he knelt beside her now and she heard his voice. "Lily, my love, are you all right?"

With her throat parched from screams she croaked, "John Roxbury, is it really you?"

"Yes, Lily, it's me, it's John."

"Oh, John Roxbury, what took you so long?"

As he held his blue-eyed girl in his arms he knew he was finally home. As she cradled her head into the hollow of his shoulder, she knew she was in the special niche where only she was destined to fit.

"I love you, Lily Abrams."

"I love you, John Roxbury."

# FINDING LILY

When their eyes met in that first moment of familiarity, they both experienced a union too many years overdue. They both knew they had loved each other since before they were born, at least it seemed that way. The deafening roar encompassing them, lifted them to a realm of existence where they had been personally joined together by the hands of fate. They knew where they belonged, they always had. When John lowered his gaze to Lily's rosebud lips he knew he did not have to claim her, she was already his. Lily placed her hands on John's cheeks, drawing him toward her. As their lips met they knew it was to finally seal the unspoken pact between them.

Lily thought she would die. Her heart no longer beat as hers. Each thump became a metronome with his until the two hearts beat as one. She could not help but cry out with joyfulness. She could not believe she was finally in the arms of her love. She was overwhelmed by the pure wonder of it all.

John felt as weak as a newborn babe. He had never felt such an overpowering need to be loved. He would have walked over embers to the end of the earth just to experience this one moment in time, a moment in an ageless universe. He felt like a wind god had just performed the act of creating him and he had just opened his eyes for the first time. With that act of seeing, he had just laid eyes on the most beautiful living thing, and she was his.

They wanted nothing more than to stay in each other's arms all day. They had so much to talk about, so many years to make up. It would take days for each to tell their stories, but John insisted on taking Lily home to the safety of her father. There was also the matter of the scoundrel who lay as a heap of rubbish. John planned to tie him to a tree, take Lily home and return to escort him to the jailhouse. If the sheriff wanted to talk to Lily he could do it tomorrow.

"Come on, Lily, I'll take you home."

"Oh, John Roxbury, I can't leave you now, I've only just found you."

John liked the habit Lily had always had of calling him by his first and last name. "Lily, I know you remember me as John Roxbury, but my name is Horn now, it has been for several years."

"Why on earth did you change your name, John Roxbury—I mean John Horn?"

"It's a long story and I'll tell you later. Right now I need to get you home to your father and come back for this coot. He'll remember what happened when he wakes up in jail."

"But— "

As John finished binding the ruffian to a tree he said, "But nothing, Lily, come on with me." John took Lily's dainty hand in his. As they once again looked into each other's eyes they affirmed their love for each other.

"I love you, Lily Abrams."

"I love you, John Horn."

He led her away from the once peaceful setting that had just a few minutes earlier become a place of peril. Lily clung to the bodice of her dress with her free hand, holding it together as best she could. Her chemise modestly covered her breasts. As John guided her back through the trail he thought of the future he hoped to have with Lily.

Lily, on the other hand, was struggling with the inevitable outcome of this incident. Her father would be furious. He had warned her many times not to go into the woods alone. He had told her the evilness of men would overpower her and her virtue would always be in danger. She was becoming a young lady and she might not understand it yet, but men would begin to find her desirable and would take advantage of her innocence if they were given the opportunity. He could not warn her enough of the dangerous consequences of being alone and vulnerable to men. Knowing her father as she did, there was no doubt he would take drastic measures to ensure this would never happen again.

As they broke through the wooded area leading to the narrow road they were met by a fuming Preacher Tom. If his parishioners could have laid eyes on him at that moment they would have experienced the wrath of God on a man's level. He was livid with rage, not very becoming for a preacher man. His eyes glared when he came eyeball to eyeball with this ruffian he'd seen on various occasions sitting on the porch of Ravenwood. He had seen him often enough sitting and talking to or arm in arm with the owner, the black-haired harlot. John would have caught on fire if the sparks that seemed to fly from Preacher Tom's eye sockets were real.

As he grabbed hold of Lily's arm he shouted, "Girl, what are you doing with this—this sinner?"

Noticing the rip in her dress he once again turned his attention toward John. "As God is my witness, I'll see you in hell if you've hurt this child."

"Daddy, it wasn't him, John stopped the man from— "

"Quiet, Lily!"

John knew he was dealing with a volatile man; preacher or not he was probably capable of physical force. John also knew if there was any chance at all of him seeing Lily again he'd have to keep his own temper in check. He quietly said, "Sir, my name is John Horn. Your daughter's screams brought me to her rescue. She's untouched. The man is tied to a tree and I plan to bring him to the sheriff. I haven't done anything to harm your daughter. You may remember me; I went to school with Lily in Mackinaw City. I was raised by Mrs. Roxbury. My sister is Moonwater, she owns Ravenwood."

John's words might have just as well fallen on deaf ears. Preacher Tom was already turning to leave, taking Lily with him. He stopped long enough to turn around and say with accusation, "I know full well whom your sister is; she's the harlot of that boarding house."

Lily sucked in her breath, agape in shock. "Daddy!"

Preacher Tom's words cut John with the precision of a finely honed straight razor. He felt the cutting remark slap across his face and draw blood. He felt the blood trickle down his cheek where in contrast, moments earlier, he had felt the love and warmth of Lily's slight hands. This so-called man of God was nothing more than a hypocrite. If he thought they were sinners, why wasn't he at least interested in trying to save their souls, instead of damning them to hellfire and brimstone?

The last vision John had of Lily was her brilliant blue-green eyes dull with pain and humiliation in her tear-streaked face. Her yellow hair hung down her back entangled with dead leaves and twigs. With head lowered she walked away with her father. John had the terrible premonition that seeing Lily was going to be next to impossible. Her words echoed in his mind as he latched onto them, opened his heart and placed them securely inside and threw away the key: "I love you, John Horn."

# NOT SO FOND FAREWELL

If Lily thought for a minute her father would get over his outburst she was sadly mistaken. The next morning he was at the dock saying good-bye to his precious daughter who held a scowl on her face and vowed never to forgive him for sending her away. The smell of the forthcoming winter was in the air and Lily felt as forsaken as the leaves of autumn as they were tossed about in the wind.

"Why now, Daddy, why would you send me away to school now?"

"It's for the best, Lily. You're a young lady now, nearly seventeen."

Lily's sobs were for naught. Preacher Tom was adamant about sending her to the girls' school in Pennsylvania. He had written a bank draft for her tuition and was sending it along with her chaperon. She would be gone for three years. He figured it would be plenty enough time for her education. It could also serve to rid her of any thoughts of this Indian drifter, John Horn. His wish was for Lily to marry a nice young doctor or attorney, certainly not an Indian scallywag.

Lily's pleas burst through his thoughts as she once again cried out, "Please, Daddy, please don't send me away. I've loved John since we were children. How can you be so cruel? I love him, Daddy, I love him!" Lily's tears streamed down her face as her voice rose in hysteria. She struggled with her chaperon until finally she was led onto the steamer

*Hunter*, which made daily trips back and forth from Manistique to Sainte Ignace. As Lily boarded, nearly collapsing with fatigue, she thought she would cease to breathe.

It broke the preacher's heart to hurt his only daughter but he knew it was for the best. He believed he was doing the right thing for her. He watched from the dock until the *Hunter* became a lone dot on the horizon. He would miss her terribly and believed with time his little girl would understand and come to forgive him.

Also watching what was taking place was Chief Ossawinamakee. He fondly remembered the girl with the mooneye. He had no way of knowing this heart-wrenching scene would be reflected in his nephew's eyes for many days. Even though John Horn had no idea yet that his Lily was being sent out East, this day would be played over in his mind, wearing him down like the path of an oxen team wore down the earth.

Semo watched as Preacher Tom walked sluggishly away from the dock. The burden on this man's shoulders weighed heavily. He carried the weight of his only child's broken heart. He knew her ache was ripping her apart, yet he strongly believed he had made the right decision and now he would live with it.

A lone tear burned a trail down Semo's cheek. His heart thudded with a resounding blast of hatred for the preacher man. He would probably burn in hell for his thoughts, but then the white man's hell was not his belief. He believed in the gods of nature and his hell had already been lived through his ancestors.

Semo also felt his own burden of having to be the one to tell John that Lily was gone. He had just spoken to John the day before when John had excitedly told him about the man who had attacked Lily in the woods. After the confrontation with Preacher Tom, he had taken the battle-scarred varmint to Sheriff Jachor, who happened to be part Indian and deaf at that. He used an ear trumpet, which John found to be a little comical. After relaying his story to Sheriff Jachor, the slightly lethargic man had been unceremoniously thrown into a cell at the local jailhouse. The sheriff promised he would be treated accordingly.

John left him and followed up on a job offer from the foreman at the Chicago Lumbering office. He had left that morning himself, his departure just a bit earlier than Lily's. John's destination was the Stutts Creek Logging Camp. They were preparing for the winter by cutting of the virgin timber. By the end of winter they would have enormous piles that had to be hauled on sleds or big wheels to the Manistique River. They used oxen and workhorses sent in from his uncle's farm. In the spring John would jump on the log run. He had no experience with the log drives but he was strong, sure-footed and a healthy, vibrant and determined young man. The foreman felt confident he would be perfect for the job and good men were cherished in this business.

John's determination came from selfish reasons. His plan was to sock away his earnings as he had done in the past. He wanted to buy a piece of property, marry Lily and raise a family. He had no idea as he entered the bunkhouse at Stutts Creek Camp that his dreams had set sail out of the Manistique Harbor.

Lily had cried herself into an exhausted heap on a cot in the captain's galley. The captain had promised to take special care of her and her chaperon. He owed Preacher Tom a favor for saving the soul of a brother he thought he'd lost to the clutches of alcohol. If not for Preacher Tom's prayers and counseling, his brother would have drank himself to death years ago. He had a deep admiration for the preacher and found Lily to be a delight. He wondered about the sorrowful girl as she now lay sleeping. He thought her grief had to lie deeper than what would come from leaving her father for the first time in her life. Her chaperon wasn't talking and Preacher Tom had only said she was going off to school. Maybe Lily would confide in him, but right now he had to tend to the duties of his crew.

# BECOMING A LUMBERJACK

John's first day at the log camp was filled with trepidation. He had taken the Haywire train to Shingleton, then hiked seven miles along the upper west branch of the Manistique River to the Stutts Creek Camp. His past job experience could not have prepared him for the duties he would now face. The logging camp housed over 800 men. They slept in rough-hewn bunks stacked three high. No one had a pillow, which would have been a luxury. The blankets were jagged cuts of heavy felt. The bunkhouse filled his nostrils with a stench that turned his stomach. Most of the men had already adapted to the smell of sweat, cigar smoke and the sour smelling tobacco spittle.

They ate in shifts; most of the meals were sowbelly, tators and plenty of bread. Several of the shanty boys were bull's eye accurate with a rifle and also provided venison to be prepared by Nelly, the camp cook. If you didn't get to the mess hall on time, you ate it cold. The men were rowdy and cussed enough to make a good man blush. Smoking cigarettes, referred to as "coffin nails," was frowned on. Most of the men chewed tobacco and spit in big spittoons or on the floor. Some smoked big black cigars, which left John with a dizzy sensation. John thought he'd pass out when his eyes started to lose focus.

All the men wore heavy woolen plaid shirts. Most of them itched continuously, but John didn't know if it was from the wool or the bedbugs that infested them. Their trousers, also woolen, were held up by suspenders and rested just above the ankle. Some of them were so filthy they could have stood up in a corner by themselves. They all had leather boots, some with calked soles. The boots all had brass eyelets and leather laces. John noticed some had slashes in them likely made by a misguided ax or cant hook.

John was having second thoughts and then remembered why he was there. He was doing it for Lily. That thought alone would be enough to keep him going with this job that would no doubt be an adventure to say the least. His thoughts wandered to his blue-eyed girl with the flowing blond hair. Her smile could bring sunshine to any drab day. Her words echoed in whispers inside his head, "I love you, John Horn."

Some of the men were playing cards in the bunkhouse. They would all turn in early, for tomorrow they would be sharpening tools, repairing sleds, cutting leather straps and clearing skid ways for the haul. John stood slightly back away from the table, watching the four men. One of them noticed him and yelled, "What you lookin' at, boy? What's yer name?"

John always used caution in any new surroundings, especially with a large group of men he didn't know. He met the man's stare and firmly stated, "Horn, the name's John Horn."

Suddenly there was an eruption of emotion and raucous laughter with high-pitched squeals. John's first thought was that there was a brawl ensuing. He was the new man in this camp and might not be accepted as readily as the regulars had been. Most of these men had been with the Chicago Lumbering Company for years now. They were seasoned to the hard life of the woods and logging camps. The log drivers were known to each other as "river hogs."

The man speaking to him jumped up from his stool, sending it to the floor with a flip. He made his way toward John, his arm outstretched for a handshake. His nearly toothless grin produced a slight dimple in his cheek, making his hardened face look boyish. His snarled hair came loose as he took his hat off. His hand made a sweeping motion, fingers combing through his blond locks as he placed his hat back on. He grabbed John's hand with a strong grip and slapped him on the back, nearly sending him sprawling to the floor.

"Well I'll be damned, boy; it's a pleasure to meet you, John Horn. I thought you were a legend. Yer the boy who grabbed a bull by the horn, threw it to the ground, broke its neck and slit its throat with yer bare hands! I'll be darned."

John's grin widened from ear to ear when he realized he was standing in a room full of men who believed one of the old stories that had been passed around years ago. Each time it was told something more outrageous was tacked onto it. He was not about to ruin the legend that had gone on for years. Recovering from the slap on the back he said, "Yep, that's me."

"My name is Paul, Paul Knuth, I'm yer foreman, boy."

After all the introductions were made the men returned to their card game and John decided to call it a night, even though the sun was still an hour from setting. He knew call out came at four in the morning, which would take some getting used to. His off time between his jobs was over and he was ready to make a fresh start with his new endeavor. He had a lot to learn and intended to eventually be the best river hog to ever come off the Manistique River.

He found his bunk, luckily a top one. He'd heard the bedbugs were so bad at times that they would drop down onto the lower bunks, and he was not used to being in such poor conditions. His days of sleeping in a luxurious bed were over. Moonwater had spoiled him with her pampering. He would definitely miss the warm comfortable bed, good home-cooked meals and of course her gracious company. The one thing he wouldn't miss were the advances of the girls she employed. They were too free with their flirting, always looking for a kiss or caress. His heart belonged to Lily and only Lily could fill the void in his lovesick heart.

He could still hear the sounds of the camp as he slipped into as much of a relaxing position as he could on the hard bunk. His thoughts went to Lily. They were always with Lily. He wondered what she was doing right now. He could see her walking in the woods, jumping over the creek, picking wild flowers, making a wreath for her luxurious hair. He could hear her tinkling voice ring out in a sweet serenade. He could hear her giggle over the antics of romping rabbits running wild in the woods, her hushed whispers to the frolicking spotted fawns. He could see her face, an expression of awe on it as she watched a mama fox playing with her pups. He tasted her sweet luscious kiss.

That first kiss had been like the sweet taste of honey on his lips. Her hair felt like silk in his fingers as the smell of lilacs drifted into his nostrils. Her innocence radiated from her delicate body. He would give anything to taste her on his lips again. He wanted to hold her in his arms forever. Sweet, sweet Lily. The image of her followed him into the realm of sleep where his dreams could capture her. *Good night, sweet Lily.*

# Ravenwood's Addition

May was making her way down the road toward the east side of town. She always enjoyed the walk. The air was crisp this morning. The days were getting shorter and the nights colder. She dreaded the winters in Manistique. The snow fell continuously, one storm after another. The banks were always piled high. Her hired man could barely keep up with the shoveling. Each year brought a new record snowfall; last winter the snowfall had exceeded 220 inches.

When the wind blew in from the southeast off the lake the streets were drifted shut, making navigation nearly impossible. She always stocked up on supplies in the wintertime. This morning, with the frosted leaves crinkling under her feet, she was on a different mission. She wanted to see if her new hat had arrived at Alice's Hat Shop. She had ordered it months ago and she hoped it would arrive before winter set in. She also had to stop at the general store. The new shipment had arrived and she planned to purchase baby garments and diaper material. She needed to stock up on nursing bottles, talcum powder, coverlets, infant day and night slips, booties; purchase a cashmere cloak; order a perambulator; and perhaps treat herself to a new perfume atomizer.

Korina, her singer and pianist, had gotten careless and was expecting a baby in January. Of course the man who had fathered it was long gone. He would never know he had a child. He was a businessman from Boston. He was a dashing man in his double diaconal worsted suit, English Kersey overcoat and derby. He was a distinguishing man with his Meerschaum pipe. He had spent the whole month of April at Ravenwood and claimed to have fallen in love with Korina. Most of the men did, some proclaimed it and some didn't. Mr. Jackson had sworn his loyalty, even promising to come back for Korina. She had believed him until she saw his picture on the society page of the *Boston Herald*. It was an engagement announcement. The beautiful blonde pictured with him was a banker's daughter. How could a man go wrong? Beauty and money was the best of both worlds.

Korina had cried for weeks. May feared she would lose the baby in her early months. The doctor insisted she get as much rest as she could and stay off her feet as much as possible. Finally Korina accepted the fact that Mr. Jackson was a gold-digger and had used her for an idiot. By the time her belly was swollen with Mr. Jackson's baby he was off to Europe on a honeymoon paid for by his new father-in-law.

May had already renovated a room at Ravenwood. It would be perfect for a nursery. Having a baby around the girls would keep them all amused and serve as a reminder for them to use protection. Her handyman had handcrafted a walnut cradle and a rocking chair which would most likely be in continuous use. Everyone was looking forward to having a turn at being a godmother. May was across town faster than usual, lost in her daydreams.

"My my, aren't you the beautiful one today!"

May was snapped back to reality by the unmistakable voice of her uncle. "Uncle Semo, how are you? I nearly walked right past you!"

Semo laughingly joked, "I know, child, and I thought you were blinded."

"Come have lunch with me, Uncle, we have so much to catch up on."

"I'd be delighted, Moonwater."

"I just have to stop in at the hat shop and pick up some things at the general store, then I'll meet you at the restaurant."

"I was on my way to the livery station; I'll meet you in a half hour."

Moonwater hugged her uncle and hurried off to Alice's Hat Shop. When she entered the store Mrs. Clark was bustling around giving orders to the shopkeeper. She didn't hear the tinkling of the bell over the door. The young clerk was flustered around her; she was such a demanding customer. Mrs. Clark spent a great deal of money in town and the storeowners kowtowed to her every whim. She was known to be the town gossip and had a following of a few who reveled in it. For most others it was embarrassing when she would prattle on about everyone. Her unfortunate subject this morning was Korina.

"… well I never. What is becoming of this good town? The likes of that young girl getting herself pregnant! That boarding house is a disgrace to this town. All the carrying on over there with all those men. Why, Preacher Tom said to me just yesterday— "

May stood directly behind Mrs. Clark and in her sensuous voice spoke to the back of the woman's head, "Good morning to you, Mrs. Clark."

Mrs. Clark turned around and her face drained of color. Her mouth flew open to say something but May did not give her the chance. "Mrs. Clark, who do you think you are? You have the mouth of a venomous snake!"

The sales clerk's hand flew to cover her mouth so the laughter that sparkled in her eyes could not escape her mouth. It was about time someone shut this woman up. The busybody was of no use to anyone. The clerk liked May; she shopped often and bought all the girls' dresses and hats from her. She spent nearly as much money as Mrs. Clark did. She made herself busy, trying not to draw any more attention to Mrs. Clark than the woman deserved.

Mrs. Clark finally recovered her wits and spat out an obscenity at May, trying to brush past her to get out the door. May would not be badgered by this woman any longer. She was long overdue for a good tongue-lashing, but May knew a better way to get Mrs. Clark's goat.

"Mrs. Clark, how is your niece doing these days? I heard she's had another illegitimate child, and that nephew of yours, is he still in jail for fighting over at the saloon? Oh, and isn't your sister the one having an affair with Mr. Peacock? By the way…"

Mrs. Clark threw her package down, harrumphed her way past May and stamped across the floor in a huff. As always, she had to have the last word. She shrieked at May, "You are nothing but a bawd!"

As the bell tinkled on the door, in a very lady-like manner May offered, "You have a good day now, Mrs. Clark."

The sales clerk could not contain her composure any longer and burst out with laughter, giving May the feeling of being a mischievous little girl again. She was not normally a rude person, but Mrs. Clark had gotten the best of many people and she had dirt on her own back porch that needed to be swept. She had no right to treat people the way she did and May felt vindicated in speaking of things Mrs. Clark thought no one knew about. It wouldn't shut the woman up, but it would serve for the moment.

May collected her purple velvetta hat, stopped at the general store, made her purchases and continued on to the restaurant that was connected to the livery stable and Heffron's Saloon. Uncle Semo was waiting out front. The raven-haired beauty linked her arm through his and as they entered the restaurant, his stately presence filled the room. Heads turned at the sight of the statuesque Indian chief and the petite and poised owner of the only brothel in town. Men gawked while women leered and made whispered catty remarks. It didn't bother either one of them as Semo stared back with a smile on his hard-edged face and Moonwater held her head high and confident.

They sat at a table near a window and each enjoyed a roast beef sandwich and homemade vegetable soup. Oblivious to their surroundings, their conversation was private as they talked about life. Semo chuckled when he learned about the expectation of a baby at Ravenwood. That would no doubt be the talk of the town. In 1892 babies born out of wedlock were unmentionable but would spur many hushed whispers from the town biddies. May told him Mrs. Clark already had a good start, but might be tongue-tied for a few days. His booming laughter could be heard throughout the restaurant.

Tears swam in May's eyes when she learned of Lily's unexpected journey on the *Hunter*. Just a month ago John had said his goodbyes on the front step of Ravenwood. He had been elated and hopeful for a chance at a life with Lily. Semo expected him back in town in a few weeks. Most of the logging crew would be making a final trip to town before winter. Some would collect their pay and head for the saloons, some would stock up on supplies, some would go to church and others would come for a visit. Semo would have to tell John about Lily and he was not looking forward to his task. Moonwater was discouraged about the twist of fate her brother's life had taken, again. Was he never going to be able to live his dream?

•

# KITCHITIKIPI DREAM

Lily could do nothing but mope in her room. She had flopped onto her bed an hour ago. She had no desire to read, let alone retain what she was expected to read. The exam was tomorrow but she simply did not care. Her English instructor, Miss Wallace, was pleasant enough. She was only five years older than Lily. It was her first job and she tried to make her lessons fun while spilling the vessel of knowledge into her classroom. She was highly respected, having come from a long line of rich landowners. Her father's money had paid for the best possible education she could acquire. He also made yearly donations to the school. He was proud of her career, admiring her from afar.

Lily's roommate was a bratty girl. She came from a rich family also and was an only child. Unlike Lily, she was spoiled beyond repair. Suzanne did nothing but whine. She whined about the food, her bed was too hard, her pillow too soft, the room too cold, the library had too many steps to climb and there weren't nearly enough windows to look out. She had an endless stream of complaints. Lily didn't want to be mean, but she silently wished her roommate would just shut up!

Lily replayed the scene on the dock. It was hard to believe two months had passed. The *Hunter* had docked in Sainte Ignace, she'd spent the night at the hotel, boarded the train for Pennsylvania and here she was, stuck in a school with teachers, books, lessons and snotty girls. All she wanted was to be with John Horn. She knew she would never forgive her father for sending her away. She couldn't comprehend how her life had changed overnight.

She had always been Daddy's little girl. He had never been overprotective of her. He had always allowed her to be herself. He had instilled good moral decency in her, which would never change. What had hardened his heart?

"Liillly, where is my yellow drresss?" Suzanne's high-pitched whiny voice interrupted her thoughts. Lily grit her teeth and kept her face turned toward the wall. *Maybe if I ignore her she'll go away*, she thought.

Suzanne whined again, "Liilly can you heearr meee?"

*How can I not hear you*, Lily thought.

"Wheerre's my yellloow dreesss?"

Lily had had it. Sitting up in bed she shouted at Suzanne, "Will you please shut your whining mouth and just go away!"

Suzanne's eyes bulged in surprise. Her mouth flew open and for once she was speechless. She certainly never expected anything malicious to come out of Lily's pure mouth. Suzanne knew Lily was a preacher's daughter and she secretly thought of her as a Miss goody-two-shoes. Lily was normally a soft spoken and genteel girl; her outburst and onslaught of cruelty surprised Suzanne. Her voice went up an octave or two as she ran out of the room crying and screaming. "Miss Waalllace, Liillly's shouting at mmeee!"

Lily threw herself back onto the bed, staring at the ceiling as tears spilled from her stinging eyes and fell onto her already tear-stained pillow. She had cried so many tears she thought a dam had burst in her tear ducts. How was she ever going to make it through the next three years? Her thoughts went unspoken. *Where are you, John Horn?*

As her body relaxed she drifted into the realm of dreams where only she and John existed *holding her close to his muscular body, they escaped from the threat of her father. They walked through a trail in the woods on the other side of Indian Lake in Manistique. They came upon a clearing in the woods where the most beautiful sight lay before them. The crystal clear water of the spring reflected the color of the sky. They watched as aged fish swam in schools. These fish were so large they seemed gigantic as the water magnified their bodies. White sand bubbled up from the underground springs in a continuous rhythmic dance. Trees had fallen over along the edge and lay on the bottom, creating a magical illusion. They drifted in a canoe in the middle of the spring where overhanging branches of lush green cedar trees swayed in the warm gentle summer breeze. The reflection of the trees on the mirror-like surface frolicked in whimsical play. They kissed and proclaimed their love for each other, making a pact for life. They felt the presence of Wahwahtaysee and Young Eagle who many years before had proclaimed their undying love in much the same way. Legend told of the two young Indian lovers who had met at the spring called Kitchitikipi. Wahwahtaysee's father had forbidden her to be with Young Eagle, as she was already promised to a chieftain. While climbing into the canoe from an outstretched branch Wahwahtaysee had fallen into the water. Young Eagle had jumped in to save her and they had both lost their lives in the grips of the icy water. Their petrified bodies lay at the bottom of the spring, together forever in the eternal depths. On a clear day their bodies could be seen holding each other in a fossilized immortal embrace.*

Kitchitikipi is an Indian word meaning "mirror of heaven." Lily's dream took her into the scope of that heaven.

*The wild flowers filled her senses with a sweet jasmine perfume. The songbirds lilt filled the air. The warm breeze caressed her body as John Horn was caressing her with his hands. She felt her spirit delicately melting into his with each kiss. They would never be separated again. Her name was on his lips as he placed tiny kisses on her neck and face. Lily, Lily, Lily…*

"Lily, Lily, wake up—Lily, wake up."

Lily fought to stay in her dream world but she was persistently being dragged back to the reality where she did not wish to be. Through the ebbing fog of sleep she heard Miss Wallace's words, "Lily, wake up."

She fought to focus her eyes and face the fact she was not in John Horn's arms. As she burst into tears again Miss Wallace held her to her breast and allowed her to cry her torrent of melancholy tears. Miss Wallace feared she would never be able to console Lily. She feared this pining girl would never get over the ache that held her heart in a deathtrap. When Suzanne told her about Lily's outburst she knew she was not herself and something must be done. She was sending for a doctor tomorrow.

"Oh, Lily, let it out, honey, cry your heart out, you sweet miserable girl."

"Oh, Miss Wallace, I fear I will die without John Horn. I love him with all of my being. I feel I will die if I can't be with him."

"I understand, Lily, I really do understand."

Miss Wallace held Lily until she once again fell into a deep sleep. She covered her with the soft coverlet, wiped the fresh salty tears from her cheeks and quietly tiptoed across the room. Her heart went out to this fragile girl who reminded her of herself.

It was just two years since she had lost her own precious love. She knew no man would ever be good enough for her in her father's eyes. If it hadn't been for an elderly auntie consoling and counseling her through it, she would still be in the same condition Lily was in right now. Her father had sent her love on a treacherous trek across the northern mountains of California on the supposition of a land scheme. He had met with a terrible accident when his horse slipped over the edge of a narrow precipice. Miss Wallace never would have known what had happened if not for her uncle who was in a nearby town when an old miner had brought the news to town.

After grieving his death for over a year she had made the strenuous journey out east. She was able to forgive her father, but she knew she would never forget and would never be able to look at her father with the same respect he had taught her. She knew her father made monetary contributions to the school and she was thankful, but she also knew he was trying to pacify his guilt. Miss Wallace knew exactly what Lily was feeling and it broke her heart to witness it. She vowed to be her counselor and friend and treat her like a little sister who was so in need of an understanding advisor.

"Sleep now, Lily, and sweet dreams."

# MIDNIGHT DELIVERY

A pain-filled scream resounded through the night air at the Ravenwood. May was out of bed and on her feet running down the hallway between the rooms. She knew the scream had come from Korina. The last week had been rough on her. Her belly had swollen to a tremendous size. She lay in bed moaning most days, feeling the uncomfortable kicking and rolling of her baby. The pressure was almost unbearable for her. Just two days earlier the doctor had told her the baby would be born any day. He had told May to send for him at the first sign of labor. He felt there would be problems because of Korina's small hips and the size of the baby.

As May reached the door to Korina's room, she saw that one of the other girls was already there. Quickly May told her to fetch the doctor. As she turned and ran down the stairs May entered the room. Korina lay on her bed writhing in agony. Her face was flushed as sweat ran down her forehead. She was clutching the end of her coverlet, balling it up in her fist. The fear in her eyes struck May with apprehension. She certainly could not let on she was afraid too. Korina needed someone to help her tolerate her pains and give her the confidence she needed for the birth of her baby.

"I'm here, Korina, please just try to relax. Missy has gone for Doctor

110

Walker." May quickly poured some water into a basin and dipped a cloth into the cool water. She wiped Korina's brow and face as she began to calm. She felt hot to the touch and May feared she was running a fever. The doc had said there might be complications, but what those complications might be, May did not know.

"That's a good girl, just try to relax now."

May felt Korina's body tighten again as she was gripped with another pain. She arched her back, raising her protruding belly off the bed with a wail. "Oh, May, it hurts, it hurts so awful."

"You'll be fine; the doctor will be here soon. I'm right here with you, I won't leave you, Korina." God, she hoped the doctor would be here soon. It should only take a short time to get across town with the horse and surrey. The doctor would be prepared to just throw his clothes on, grab his bag and race back across town. May knew the few minutes would seem like an eternity. Korina was relaxing again when there was a faint tapping on the bedroom door. As May turned, two of the other girls came in with some hot water and linen for the delivery. They had all been preparing for what to do when the time arrived.

"How is she, May? Have you sent for the doctor?"

May instructed the girls to ready what the doctor would need for the delivery. "Yes," she said, "Doctor Walker should be here in a few minutes, now if you want to stay, at least sit quietly."

The girls were young and most of them had no experience with babies being born. May didn't either, for that matter. She remembered when her mother had given birth to John but she was not there to witness the actual birth. She really didn't know the full scope of a birth. Indian women seemed to be tougher when it came to those things. They knew how to channel their pain and capture a peaceful nature to help them cope. May had a feeling this was going to be an entirely different episode.

Missy rushed breathlessly into the room. "Doctor Walker is here, May; he's on his way up."

"Thank you, Missy, now please sit quietly with the other girls. If we need you we'll let you know."

Missy joined Tessa and Lydia as they all sat wide-eyed and

whispered amongst themselves. They were so excited with anticipation of a baby but they were apprehensive of the ordeal Korina would have to endure to make this miracle happen.

"How is she, May?" Doctor Walker asked as he entered the room.

"She's in a great deal of pain, Doctor, and I think she's running a fever, she seems awfully hot. I've been mopping her down with cool water. I'm so afraid for her, Doctor."

As Doctor Walker opened his bag and took out a small bottle of liquid, Korina again contorted with another severe pain. She let out an agonizing scream, spontaneously making the three girls in the corner gasp and cry out. They held each other's hands and pulled together in a huddle for support. Just as May was having second thoughts about letting them stay Doctor Walker turned and said, "The girls will have to leave, May, this is not going to be a pleasant birth."

He didn't have to repeat himself; Missy, Tessa and Lydia were already scurrying out the door. Tessa turned and said, "You'll let us know when the baby comes, won't you, May?"

"Yes, I'll let you know. Go heat some more water on the stove and bring it to me, then I suggest you go to your rooms and say a prayer."

Doctor Walker had checked Korina to see how the progression of the birth was coming along. It was as he had feared—the baby was big and Korina's birth canal was too small. This was going to be a very difficult birth. He silently hoped this young girl was strong enough to see it through to the end. She had already started to open up inside and was lying in a pool of water, which meant it wouldn't be long now. Her pains would be coming harder, longer and with less time in between. Another scream filled the room as Korina shouted, "It hurts so bad, I feel like I'm going to die! Can't you do something, Doctor?"

Doctor Walker poured a glass of the clear liquid, held the back of Korina's head up and, placing the rim of the glass on her bottom lip, said, "Drink this, Korina, it will help with your pain. I'm right here, everything will be fine."

She swallowed the bitter fluid and, closing her eyes, fought with the beginning of another pain traveling across her abdomen with an intense contraction. She began to tremble when she felt the weight of a heavy boulder pushing through her insides, trying to get out. She felt she was being stretched beyond possibility. She screamed again as May held her hand, trying to sooth the spirit of this terrified girl. May felt entirely feeble as she watched Doctor Walker spread Korina's legs and place pillows under them to prop them up. Examining her again he said, "Korina, now listen to me. Your baby's head has moved down, with your next pain I want you to try pushing as hard as you can and help push this— "

Before he could finish his sentence she was struck with a lightening hot pain. She felt like something burning had been pushed up inside of her. Her belly tightened with pain again and she desperately tried to do what the doctor had told her. She gave a mighty push and screamed into the night. Her tender skin had stretched to its limit and she felt a scalding sensation as her already tender skin ripped from the pressure of the baby's head passing through. Missy entered the room, bringing hot water, and dashed back out as fast as she could. She told herself she would never have a baby if this was what she'd have to go through.

"All right, Korina, just one more push, dear, your baby's head is out, as soon as the shoulders are out your baby will be here."

Doctor Walker couldn't believe the baby looked to be so small. There was no reason for the mother to be having such severe pains, more severe than for a normal birth. His thoughts nagged at him but he concentrated on Korina as he felt her belly contract with another pain.

"One more push now, Korina, and your baby will be here."

May was holding Korina's hand and wiping her brow with the cool clothe. She felt so vulnerable, but knew if she kept busy she could get herself and Korina through this. The miracle of this birth was pulling on her heartstrings and she felt privileged to be able to observe it. She knew she would be exhausted by the time morning came.

She watched in astonishment as a wet and bloodied baby slid out into the doctor's skilled hands. He cleaned her nostrils and mouth out, held her upside down and after he whacked her on her tiny buttocks, the baby let out a faint cry. The baby was so small, weighing barely five pounds, but she looked perfectly intact. May watched as Doctor Walker tied off and cut the cord that connected her to her mother. He handed the precious newborn to May and instructed her to wash her off with warm water and wrap her in a tiny quilt.

As the doctor once again turned his attention to Korina for the cleanup process that came after the birth, she was suddenly gripped with a pain that had her screeching again. He felt her abdomen and his face dropped with the realization of his nagging perception—there was another baby. Now he knew why her pains were unusually extreme, and he was faced with the fear of what could happen if the second baby did not come as easily as the first.

"May, I need your help, there's another baby."

May was shocked. "What, another baby? How can that be?"

"It's twins, May. I thought there was a possibility of it because she was so big but there was no way of knowing until now." He lowered his voice so Korina could not hear. "If this second baby doesn't come as easily as the first I may lose her."

May's stunned heart jumped. "Lose her, what do you mean. Doctor?"

"Korina is starting to lose blood. If this baby is bigger, which I fear it is, it will be harder for her to push it out; her insides won't open wide enough for a big baby. She can't afford to lose any more blood."

May's head was swirling with panic as she tearfully whispered, "Korina may die?"

Trying to ignore the dread in her voice he said, "Korina may die and the other baby may die or have problems too."

Looking at Korina's weakened condition, for the first time in his profession he felt powerless. He hoped the girls were praying in the next room because he was going to need all the help from above he could get.

"Get one of the girls to boil more water for me. Don't say anything about this; I don't want them to worry. Just tell them she has a baby girl and we're making her comfortable."

May walked down the hall in a daze. She felt like someone had just released a plug from the top of her head and all the life was escaping from her. She wanted to break down and cry, but knew both Korina and the doctor needed her. For once in her life she did not want to be strong. She wanted to throw herself to the floor and cry out to the spirits to take her misery and throw it to the god of the wind. She was so angry she wanted to smash her fist into the wall and scream at the top of her lungs. She was angry with Mr. Jackson for getting Korina pregnant, she was angry with Korina for getting pregnant, she was angry at the world right now and she was even angry with the white man's god. "How could this happen?" she spoke out loud. Still, she silently prayed, *Dear God, please don't let Korina die.*

# THE GIFT OF LIFE

As May neared the bedroom where the girls were waiting she tripped over a rug. She fell onto her knees, crying out in pain as she hit the hardwood floor. She slumped forward, burying her face in her hands, and let out a wail filled with such painful sorrow it brought the girls running to her.

"May, are you all right? May, did you hurt yourself? Is Korina okay? Did she have the baby yet?" Tessa, Missy and Lydia were all speaking at once and their voices seemed to echo out from a distant place inside May's head. All she could do was sob with unstoppable distress. She was fighting to regain her composure; she knew she had to call on her inner spirit for strength. She chastised herself with a reprimanding slap to her subconscious, snapping her out of her despair.

"I'm fine, I just tripped. I need one of you to boil some more water. Korina has a baby girl, they're both fine. We're just trying to make her comfortable and clean her up. Please, just boil the water and leave it outside the door. Let me know when it's there." May gave the instructions Doctor Walker had told her to and hurried back to Korina's room.

Doctor Jeremiah Walker was an elderly man with white hair and a smallish mustache. He was usually jovial, always ready with a perky joke

116

to set his patients at ease. His bright blue eyes were always filled with mischief, but as May looked into those eyes now, she saw a very tired and harried man who had aged ten years. He did not even try to hide his anguish as May approached the bedside.

What she saw struck her with a fear closer to terror than she'd ever been in her life. Her insides lurched. She felt vomit slide up the back of her throat. Swallowing it, she choked back a scream that was trying to escape from her very soul. She started to tremble and felt her eyes bulging from their sockets. The scene before her began to swim as her tears distorted her vision. Her skin began to crawl with a cold clammy sweat. She heard a thundering reverberation in her head as she felt herself slipping to the floor, sparkles of light flashing from all sides at once. Grasping the bedpost she held on with whitened knuckles.

Korina lay in a pool of blood, dark and sticky with the faint odor of musk. Her protruding stomach had been sliced open like a butchered deer. An ugly mass of blood vessels and tissue lay between her legs. A bloody cord was still attached to a baby; at least it appeared to be a baby. It was a bundle with arms, legs, torso, head and everything else that was a baby, but this bundle was a terrible dark blue, almost black in color. It was a lifeless form.

May sensed death standing beside the bed waiting to capture its prey. *Dear God in heaven, what has happened?* May stood in horror as she watched Doctor Walker working on the baby. He was clearing out all the air passages, massaging his heart. Yes, this baby was a boy. May tried to concentrate on the doctor's efforts to revive the baby. She tried not to look at the agonized face of the now dead Korina. The beautiful pianist with the sweet lilting voice that sang in harmony would now be singing with the angels of heaven. May knew it would take more than prayers to change this scene. It would take an impossible miracle.

After a strenuous effort by Doctor Walker, May heard the faintest whimper. She sprang into action and handed him a warm cloth to wash away the blood that was beginning to dry on the baby. The baby's faint whimper soon developed into a forceful wailing. His arms started flailing and his legs kicked with a determination to come into a world he almost didn't live to see. Doctor Walker tied and cut the cord that had served as his lifeline for the last nine months. A fatigued and downtrodden man handed May the baby, gently urging her to take care of him.

"I'm sorry, May, I had no choice. Korina was losing blood so rapidly she would never have survived. I had to take the baby from her and this was the only way. It was either lose both of them or try to save the baby as quickly as I could." Dismay and grief weighed heavily on Doctor Walker as he turned to attend to Korina. He gently stitched her wound closed, washed the blood from her body and wrapped her in a clean white linen sheet. As he lowered his head his tears dropped onto the still form of Korina. In his forty years of practice he had only lost four patients. Korina was the most heartrending. He was overwhelmed.

May quieted the baby boy, laid him beside his sleeping sister and turned to console Doctor Walker. He stood near Korina's bedside, tears now streaming down his face, shoulders trembling, wracked with the release of the last six hours of his effort, which to him ended futilely. She could not begin to comprehend what he must now be feeling.

"You did everything you could, Doctor, but God had a different plan. I believe whenever someone dies a new life begins. We can never begin to understand the depth of God's love, and I believe that with all my heart. Korina is gone but her life will go on in her babies. For everything bad, something good can come to us. You're a skilled doctor and a wonderful man and you must believe this was out of your hands. A terrible thing happened here, as did a miracle. I believe what the missionaries taught me years ago: God is a God of love."

"Thank you, May. You're an amazingly strong woman, you know. I never would have been able to do without your help tonight. Korina wanted me to tell you she was proud of you too. Towards the end she knew she wasn't going to survive but she was not afraid. She just wanted me to save her baby. She also said she wanted to name the girl after you. Her name is Rebekah May."

Doctor Walker and May made their way across the room and stood over the peacefully sleeping babies, a petite and fair-skinned little girl with blond hair, barely five pounds and a hefty dark-skinned black haired boy, who was nearly nine pounds. The contrast between them made a strikingly beautiful portrait.

"Doctor, would you mind if I name the boy Jeremiah?"

Doctor Walker's face lit up with pride just as the rising sun peeked its way through the curtains. "I'd like that very much, May."

The thought struck May out of the blue: *What am I going to do with these babies?*

# BITTENEAR AND LOST ACRES

The snow in the woods around Stutts Creek Logging Camp was damn near as high as the mountainous piles of white pine logs piled along the riverbank. John had been slaving and learning the ropes of the logging trade for the past three months. Trudging through the heavy snowfall was a task in itself. The skid ways had to be kept clear of snow so the sleds and wheels could be driven back and forth with the heavy loads. Some days a wooden sleigh equipped with a water sprinkler would be used to ice the skid way. The horses were easy to handle, not so with the oxen that got a stubborn streak from time to time.

He was keen with a crosscut saw and double bitted ax. Each man had his own personal ax and treated it like a cherished woman. It had to fit just right with all the elements of perfection. The balance, weight, hang, length and thickness of the handle had to become a part of the lumberjack. The blades were sharpened each night or early morning. They were honed to razor sharpness and one blade had to be sharper than the other was. John was becoming comfortable with his surroundings when he was in the open atmosphere of the forest. He wished he could say the same for the bunkhouse.

John was more in tune with nature and felt smothered while indoors. The stench of the bunkhouse wasn't any better than when he had first arrived. There was plenty enough to eat but the boys got rowdy over card games and arguments broke out, friendly or otherwise. John, always an observer, wasn't much for gambling. Once in awhile they'd have target practice just for fun, but they always turned in their guns to Nelly, the camp cook, afterwards. With all the variations in personalities they couldn't take the chance of any of them settling an argument fatally.

John would take occasional walks into the woods to refresh his spirit and stay in tune with nature and the Indian gods he believed in. He listened to the voices of the wind, his ancestors stirring ancient memories. He reveled in the moon shadows, shadows cast on the snow as spirit clouds of the chieftains would pass before the moon. He was comforted to see a grandmother with her cooking pot on the surface of the moon. White men referred to the markings as the man in the moon. He preferred the Indian version. The crisp frosty air would fill his nostrils, feeling like crystals forming and melting, the touch of the medicine man. He was in touch with himself and the night spirits.

He thought often of the trip he had taken to Manistique just before winter set in. His visit with Uncle Semo had been like a bad dream. When his uncle had told him about Lily's departure, he felt the fist of death lunge in and try to strangle his heart. He didn't know how many more twists and turns he could take from the god of fate who was nothing more than a ruthless slug. He pictured Preacher Tom walking hand in hand with that slug. Why did love have to be so cruel? How much more would he have to endure for this endless and pain-filled love? He could only imagine the devastation Lily felt.

He had visited with Uncle Semo and Moonwater, made a few stops in town and made his way back along the Haywire Trail to Shingleton, trekked into the camp and now here he was, three months later, still wondering. How could he survive the next three years without laying an eye or hand or his lips on Lily? It wasn't in his nature to cry but his anxiety weighed heavily on him when his mind wandered to her. He did not feel complete without her near. If he'd never found her and held her in his arms the pain would be bearable, but this was beyond human cruelty. He didn't want to hate, but it boiled through his blood.

The men knocked off early one day so John decided to step into a pair of bear paw snowshoes and hike through woods toward the Duck

Creek. The logging operation would be moving that way soon and he wanted to scope it out. He packed a canteen of water and a few scrapes of bread and beef jerky. Walking along one of the well traveled trails he ran into a slough. It was a sanctuary where the deer were yarded up. Taking a winding trail off the deer path he came up over a ridge and spotted another pathway. He figured it would take him back around in a circle to the logging camp.

Halfway down the trail he spotted smoke rising above the treetops. Never being in that vicinity of the woods before, he was not prepared for what he stumbled across. It was a roughly hewn shack. A large pile of wood told him it was occupied. Carcasses of small animals hung in the tree branches in various states of decomposition. Animal fat and seed bags hung like ornaments. Against the contrast of the white snow brightly colored birds picked at the bones, tearing flesh away. The blue jay, cardinals, woodcocks, chickadees and finch were all a wonder to behold.

As he neared the shack he caught a movement with his sharp eyes. Sitting in front of the shack on a ramshackle old chair, blending in with the exterior of the shack, was an old man. His majestic face told the story of his heritage, the deep creases on weather-beaten thick dark skin could only be the face of on Indian. His hair hung long and uneven, streaked with white and a mousy black. A strap of leather encircled his forehead and tied in the back. The beads on the end rested on his shoulder. His eyes were black and produced a hard marble stare. He wore a buckskin jacket with a rabbit fur collar and buckskin leggings with fringe on the pockets, also beaded. The only thing out of place was the thick-soled leather boots on his feet.

John, not feeling threatened, said, "Afternoon to ya, sir."

"You lost?"

John took a few more steps until he stood in front of the old man. "No sir, I'm over at the logging camp on Stutts Creek, name's John Horn."

"Well, I'll be dipped in deer shit. You're Semo's kin."

"Yes sir, that's right," John chuckled.

"Bittenear's the name. Heard 'bout cha."

John shared a strong handshake with the old Indian. Looking around at his surroundings he was a bit dumbfounded at this old man who lived in a setting literally out in the middle of nowhere. The beauty and tranquility of it seemed so out of place he felt like he had walked into an era he thought to be long gone. The shack sat in the middle of a small clearing totally surrounded by trees higher than he could crane his neck to see the tops of. The comparison made the logging camp seem stark.

"Have some 'shine?"

John could already tell this old Indian wasn't used to company; his blunt way of conversing was like that of a lonely man. "I don't drink much, sir, but a little 'shine would sure warm me up right now."

Gesturing to a jug shoved into the side of a snow bank, the old man said, "Help yerself, pull up a stump."

John poured himself a generous helping of moonshine. Moonshine wasn't a sipping drink, so he took a long draw off the clear liquid, tasting the strong but smooth alcohol taste. As it traveled over the back of his throat it poured into his stomach like hot molten lava. The effect was immediate as the warmth of a pot-bellied stove filled his innards. He took in a precautiously slow breath, savoring the warm glow he was already experiencing.

"That's some mighty fine 'shine, sir."

The old Indian smiled with pride. "Made it myself."

Curious, John asked, "Have you lived out here long?"

"Been here since 1833, named this place Lost Acres."

John pulled up a stump and sat at Bittenear's feet. Bittenear told the history of how he came to settle there in the middle of nowhere. In 1813, when he was five, his father had been killed at the battle of the Thames in Ontario. American troops were attacked by a British-Indian force. The Indians were led by Tecumseh. The following year his mother died of cholera. He was living with an uncle when the battle of Mackinac Island broke out. The Americans were again defeated by a British-Indian force.

In 1815 William Henry Puthuff was the Indian agent and the American Fur Company was trading furs on Mackinac Island. They also were trading blankets and knives for Indian goods including rush mats, moccasins and shot pouches. In 1823 Henry Schoolcraft married Wabojeeg, a daughter of a Chippewa Indian chief. She taught him the language and helped him with his study of the culture and folklore. The Indians made money by selling maple syrup and porcupine quill baskets. In the summertime they traveled to the area of Epoufette fishing herring, trout and whitefish, using spears and gill nets. In the wintertime they trapped marten, otter, muskrat and beaver, trading the furs to the white man.

In 1832 Father Frederick Baraga left the Mackinac area to establish a mission church at Indian Lake in Manistique. Bittenear traveled with him, helped build the church, then moved on to where he then settled on his piece of land. John was amazed at the man's story and the detail Bittenear put into it. From his previous short answers, John didn't think Bittenear could relay a story with so many words.

John shared with Bittenear who he was. They talked about his Uncle Semo; John learned that the church Bittenear helped build was in the vicinity of Uncle Semo's horse farm. It was getting late and for a moment, time stood still.

Lost in thought for a while, Bittenear finally looked at John and said, "My last living relative is Coggogewas. In 1863 President Lincoln granted him twenty-seven acres of land in Watersmeet. One of the few times I've left this paradise was back in 1865 when I went for a visit."

John didn't realize the sun had sunk into the west until the night owl and whippoorwills started hooting and singing their songs. By this time he knew he had found a friend and felt like kin. When he got up to leave, Bittenear invited him to stay the night. "It's too dangerous in these woods at night; the wolves will eat you alive. You're more than welcome to stay, I have an extra bunk."

John accepted his invitation and in the morning when he was preparing to leave for his trek back to the logging camp and his day of work, Bittenear invited him back and that is where John Horn would spend the next three years. He had a faithful companion and mentor, and was able to escape the rugged life in the logging camp. Each day the job got nearer to Bittenear's refuge so John's walk to work became less of a hardship for him.

# KORINA'S LEGACY

Korina was laid to rest on January 23, 1892. A quiet graveside service was attended by Doctor Walker, Chief Ossawinamakee, Chef Raoule, May, Tessa, Missy, Lydia and several of the other girls who lived and worked at Ravenwood. Some chose not to attend, wanting to remember Korina in a less remorseful way. They stayed behind to watch over Jeremiah and Rebekha. Also attending were Jake, the man who had guided May to Marquette when John was attending school, and his wife Sarah. May never considered asking Preacher Tom to do the service but a kind Catholic priest learned of her death and volunteered to say a prayer over her grave, hoping that a lost soul could find her way to God.

He recited the 23rd Psalm and they all sang "Rock of Ages." The pine box was lowered into the ground, they all threw a handful of dirt and a single rose on top and said their goodbyes to Korina. They held hands and wept for the spirit of the smiling crooning girl they all knew and loved so dearly. The gravestone they had ordered was put in place by the cemetery keeper. They all placed a kiss on the top of the headstone that read simply "Korina 1872-1892—Always a Mother—Always a Friend." They thanked the priest and handed him a donation for the church which he graciously and without prejudice accepted.

When they arrived back at Ravenwood they shared a quiet dinner, after which they gathered in the lounge where one of the new girls played the piano. They all listened to, and sometimes joined in singing, all of Korina's favorite songs. There were soon wails from the babies as they made it known their need to have their diapers changed and be fed, held, rocked and loved.

May retired to her room where she could quietly contemplate and make her final decision as to the fate of Korina's babies. She had thought about it for the last two days and she closed her eyes, said a silent prayer and agreed within herself about the errand she would run in the morning. Her decision was final. She would discuss it with the girls, knowing they would all agree.

May woke early to the sounds of a blustering snowstorm. The wind was raging at a horrendous speed; snow was falling, blowing and drifting and she heard mighty cracks and snaps as branches broke off the nearby trees. Ravenwood was built strong, and only creaked and moaned a few times with the blasts of raging wind outside the windows. She made her way downstairs to have a cup of coffee with Raoule before the girls started stirring. She always enjoyed her morning chats with Raoule. She loved his stories about France and he always offered such wise advice when it came to any problems that arose.

This morning May had a heavy burden to discuss with him. She had already made her decision but she needed to hear his thoughts, and hoped too for his encouragement. They sat down to coffee and pastry and when May left the kitchen her heart was much lighter. Raoule had reinforced the wisdom in her decision and now she would tell the girls. As each one sleepily made her way into the dining room where they shared their meals, May waited until Raoule had set their breakfast of scrambled eggs, bacon and biscuits in the center of the table and retreated again to the kitchen where he would begin preparing the dinner menu.

As they began to eat and make small talk, each one subdued in thoughts of Korina, May asked if she could have all their attention for a minute. "I have something very important to discuss with all of you. Before I start, I want you all to know that I've wrestled very hard for the last several days and I've already made my own final decision, but I won't do anything without all of your approvals."

The girls sat in silence, they had never seen May so serious and concerned. They each thought their own silent thoughts. *Is she going to sell Ravenwood? Is she moving back to Mackinaw City? Is she going to ask me to leave? Is she getting married? Is she pregnant?* All of the girls had whirling thoughts. Finally Missy said, "What is it, May?"

Without hesitation, May began. "Before anyone says anything, I want you to hear me out. You all know how much I loved Korina, and I know that all of you did too. I want the best for Jeremiah and Rebekha and I'm sure all of you do too. Ravenwood is no place for babies. Our lifestyles are good and I want to run a respectable place, even though I leave it up to each of you how you entertain our guests. I want to give Jeremiah and Rebekha to Jake and Sarah. In the fifteen years of their marriage, they've tried unsuccessfully to have a baby. When Jake guided me to Marquette to see John we talked about this. It's been a burden for both of them. Sarah has been to many doctors and there is no reason why she cannot conceive a baby, yet she hasn't. Maybe this is God's way of giving them what they have both prayed for all these years."

The girls sat in stunned silence. A few tears were shed. A few heads hung low. Finally Tessa was the first to speak. "May, you know we are all family and loved Korina dearly. Having Jeremiah and Rebekha is having a part of her with us. It will sadden me to see them go, but I think you're right with this decision. None of us can be mothers right now. It's not as if we would never be able to see them and watch them grow up. I agree to your decision and I think we should have a vote right now. If you agree, raise your hand."

Missy raised her hand hesitantly, Lydia raised hers, and slowly all around the table, each girl raised her hand, giving her consent for the decision May had made for all of them. May's shoulders relaxed as she cried in relief. They all held hands around the table and unanimously agreed to give Jake and Sarah the gift that would change their lives. Jake and Sarah would have Korina's legacy.

May went to tell Raoule they would be having three guests for dinner and this would be a very special surprise dinner indeed. She sent

Missy to extend the invitation to Jake and Sarah and Doctor Walker on her behalf, making her swear to keep the secret. Missy was known for letting the cat out of the bag when it came to secrets. She swore herself to secrecy by crossing her finger over her heart saying, "I cross my heart and hope to die."

Doctor Walker arrived a bit early with Jake and Sarah arriving right on schedule for the six o'clock dinner hour. They were pleased and surprised at the invitation. They chatted and of course listened to stories about Korina. Jake and Sarah cuddled and cooed with the babies and all the girls could see the delight and longing in both their eyes. They all knew they would make wonderful parents, they just didn't know it yet.

*Ting, ting, ting* May tapped the side of her crystal wine glass with a spoon. "I would like to make an announcement."

Everyone hushed and turned their attention to the hostess. May lifted her glass in a toast. "I would like to propose a toast to Jake and Sarah, our guests."

They all raised their glasses as Jake and Sarah graciously thanked them. Doc Walker suddenly had a glint of knowing in his eyes as his heart leaped for joy.

"Jake and Sarah, we invited you to dinner with us because you are our friends, but also because we have a very special gift for you. We have all agreed on this and we want you to be the parents of Jeremiah and Rebekah."

Jake was still standing, but at this announcement he suddenly plopped into his chair. Sarah's face went ashen as tears came to her eyes; falling onto her cheeks as Jake held her with more love than any man could ever have for a woman. The girls broke out with laughter and tears as they beheld the joy of their friends. Doctor Walker walked over to May, took her hand and kissed her cheek. "You truly are a wonderful woman, May."

The evening ended with the girls helping to pack and carry out the babies' belongings. The babies were bundled up with their booties and bonnets and wrapped in warm quilts. Jake and Sarah were overwhelmed with it all. They could not believe the kind of love it took for this to happen. God had finally answered their prayers, but in the most inconceivable way. They vowed to be the best parents possible and assured the girls they would all be known as aunties to their children.

They knew a simple thank you would never be enough to express their heartfelt gratitude.

# SUMMER OF 1893

Manistique was booming in 1893 with a population of 4000. Nearby Thompson boasted a population of 500. The town was growing with stores and houses being built on a regular basis. But in the summertime tragedy struck when a fire broke at the sawmill near the river. Many of the lumberjacks were in town at the time, most being in the saloons near the area. This area near the river was referred to as the "flatiron block." It was the only area in town not owned by the Chicago Lumbering Company. A crafty man had started up a saloon and others followed suit. The saloons had billiard halls and gambling rooms.

When the raging fire started to spread rapidly and clangs of the fire wagons rang through the air, the saloons were emptied out as men rushed out the door to help. Some of the men were employed with the sawmill. They tackled the fire as if it were their own homes burning. It was engulfed in flames in no time and fighting it was near futile. Buckets of water from the river were handed from man to man and thrown onto the flames with little effect. Many of the men had to be treated by Doctor Walker for inhaling too much smoke. Many thought the whole town would burn.

By the time the fire burned itself out after being doused with thousands of buckets of water, a large portion of the sawmill, piles of lumber and fourteen buildings on the flatiron block had been destroyed, most of them saloons. Miraculously, no one lost their life in the fire. When the men, tired and blackened with soot and smoke, congregated again, it was at one of the saloons that remained standing. They watered their parched throats with beer and whisky. They stood in groups discussing their acts of fearlessness and the tragic lose.

John Horn was one of the lumberjacks in town that day and he put all his efforts into fighting the fire. Later that night at the saloon, a ruckus broke out between his foreman Paul Knuth and a man that John Horn thought he'd never have the pleasure of laying eyes on.

At a side table, five men were intent on a poker game. There was a pile of money in the center of the table. John wasn't paying much attention to it until he heard chairs flying and crashing onto the floor. The room fell to dead silence. As he turned his attention to the table he saw the face of a man contorted by a snarled sneer. Behind the sneer was a mouth with two bottom front teeth missing. John's attention immediately flew to the man's left hand, the one resting on the chest of Paul Knuth. The man stood behind him with his arm wrapped around him. It was a hand with two stubbed fingers, cut off below the second bone, blackened and grotesque.

With a lisp through yellowed teeth the man yelled, "You theated me, mithter." A knife suddenly appearing in the man's right hand was placed strategically at Paul's throat. No one moved. The man knew he was outnumbered in a room full of lumberjacks and river rats. His eyes glared fire and fear. The saloon owner inconspicuously reached behind the bar for his shotgun. He didn't know if he'd get a chance, but sure as shittin' if he did, this man was a dead man.

John's hand went to the Colt-45 on his hip. Someone suddenly shouted from behind the man and he spun around, taking Paul with him, the razor-sharp knife slicing a thin line as blood appeared. John steadily and stealthily walked up behind the man. He cocked the gun at the precise moment its barrel was placed on the man's temple. "Mister, you can kill him but you're still a dead man."

Another thin slice. Another streak of blood running down Paul's neck and onto his collar. No one moved. The air was as crisp as on a frosted morning. The tension was like the sound of crackling thin ice. John Horn's rage boiled slowly, reaching a hard rolling boil. Flashes of his mother being raped and his friend Walter being beaten to death with a board, his brains splattered in the snow went through his mind. His jaw was clenched like a bear trap. "Mister, you're dead. I'm going to tell you who I am. Name's John Horn. You beat my friend to death in Marquette over a gold watch and a poker game. You put a bullet in the chest of Chief Shawdawgun in Mackinaw City." John could see the man's hand begin to shake. He could sense his hesitation. "You raped and beat my mother and left her for dead. I see you remember now. I want you to remember my name—John Horn. Say it."

Beads of sweat formed on the man's forehead. The men stood stunned into silence. John jammed the barrel deeper into the man's temple, speaking through gritted teeth, "Say it—John Horn."

"Man, I donno whach yer talkin' 'bout, mithter."

"John Horn, say it!" he shouted. "I want the man's name who killed you to be the last word you ever speak."

The man's hand slipped ever so slightly and John took his chance. As quick as a lightening flash he transferred his Colt into his left hand and grabbed the man's wrist with his right hand, clenching until the knife started to slip. With one quick movement John grabbed the knife from the man's right hand and cut off his left hand at the wrist. The gnarled purple-black stub lay on the floor as blood spurted and the man howled like a butchered pig.

John seethed with anger and hatred, but he flatly said again, "Say my name, mister—John Horn."

"John Horn! John Horn!" The man screamed his name, holding his arm as blood continued to spurt onto the floor, spattering onto the men. Even some of the most grizzled men gagged, holding their hands over their mouths so they wouldn't puke. Some saw the quivering of the severed hand as fingers still jerked until the nerves deadened.

The man fell to the floor pleading for his life, whimpering like a baby with snot and spit running from him. None of the men had ever heard John Horn speak of these things. They knew if it were all true, which they didn't doubt it was, he was totally justified in what he was about to do. A shot rang out. The man grasped his front shoulder, screaming with agony.

"That is for Walter."

Another shot rang out. The man howled again, a wounded animal. He grasped his other shoulder, screaming and writhing with intense pain.

"That is for Chief Shawdawgun."

John Horn stood over the man, placing his Colt-45 dead center in the man's forehead.

"I am your bastard son, and this is for my mother, Star Gazer."

Most of the men had turned their backs or had silently left the saloon. The final shot rang out and the man's screams were finally silenced. Justice had spoken the final word. John Horn turned his back and walked out of the saloon, got on his horse and rode out of town to the solitude of the forest and Bittenear's humble Lost Acres.

John Horn fought with his inner spirit for many miles, reliving the scene he had just left. He didn't even bother to go see Uncle Semo or Moonwater. He knew the story would reach them soon enough. He knew Moonwater would never mention it to him and that the face that haunted her dreams would finally fade away into the dream catcher's graveyard. He had never killed a man before and was not proud of it now, even though he knew it was a justifiable act. It wasn't about revenge. It was about avenging three people's lives. One for three; the score was even now.

When he returned to Lost Acres he went into the small shack at the back where he built a fire, threw water on the heated stones and cleansed his body and spirit. He prayed to the gods of nature and knew they understood. He knew he would no longer wrestle with the inner demon. He knew the spirits of Chief Shawdawgun, Star Gazer and Walter could finally rest in peace. John Horn slept soundly that night.

# BITTERSWEET 1895

Lily's three years were nearly up. She would graduate with high honors. She had worked so hard, only looking forward to the day she would be in John Horn's arms again. She had gone through a rough time in the beginning. Miss Wallace had called in a doctor who gave her Dr. Worden's Female Pills, a blood purifier and nerve tonic. They made sure she was eating a healthy diet and getting plenty of rest. Before long Lily felt revived and her depressed spirit lifted. She tackled her studies with a new robust energy and got all A's straight through school, in all her subjects. She was proud of herself and no longer felt resentment toward her father. She missed him terribly. He had made two trips out east to see her in the three years and they had made their peace. She never asked about John Horn, she knew the subject was still a sensitive one with her father.

Lily had come to know and love her roommate Suzanne. She was a spoiled little rich girl but her whining attitude covered up a very insecure girl. She had always gotten anything she wanted, but all she really wanted was the love her parents didn't know how to give. They were both caught up in their own selfish worlds and they were worlds apart from Suzanne. Her father lived for his business dealings, always wrapped up in some new venture. He never had time for Suzanne. Her mother was just as neglected as she was and sought attention elsewhere. She secretly drank heavily and had numerous rendezvous with men.

Lily and Suzanne had shared much in three years. Lily had told her about John Horn and all their years of interruptions. She told her about her father, how he was instrumental in tearing them apart after they had finally found each other again. Suzanne told Lily about her parents, her father's business and her mother's drinking and carrying on with men. Suzanne dreamed of meeting a good man, falling madly in love and being whisked off her feet. Suzanne was such a romantic. They had shared much laughter and just as many tears. They vowed to stay in touch and Suzanne promised to name her first child after Lily, for it would surely be a girl.

Moonwater had written her several times, letting her know how John was getting along. She was proud of him for working for the Chicago Lumbering Company. By the sounds of it he was one of the top river drivers. The way Moonwater described the logging camp she was glad to hear he was staying with some character by the name of Bittenear. She knew he was happy in the elements of nature. She couldn't imagine him cooped up in a bunkhouse with 800 men.

On the day of graduation all the girls attending received a certificate of merit along with a certificate of graduation. They all enjoyed a dinner in their honor. They all expressed their well wishes and said their goodbyes. The following day each would go their separate way, some by train, some by horse and buggy and some by way of steamers or schooners. Some would remain in the area seeking positions with local businesses and some would go off to marry and raise families. Each of them would never forget the others and the last three years they had shared.

Lily arrived by schooner at the Manistique harbor. She was met by her father, and once again by the faithful greeter, Chief Ossawinamakee. As he hugged her in welcome he whispered into her ear, "John will meet you tomorrow at noon at Weber's spring." He winked and out loud he said, "Welcome home, girl with moon eye."

Smiling, Lily said, "It's nice to see you, Chief Ossawinamakee."

Lily and Preacher Tom walked hand in hand along the dock to the waiting horse and buggy. When they rode through the streets of Manistique Lily could not believe how much it had changed and grown in three years. The stoic Ossawinamakee stood as stately as she had remembered it. In addition, there were several new hotels—the Hiawatha, Tretchler Hotel, Keystone, St. James and the Hotel Barnes. She noticed the addition of several saloons and clothing stores and a shoe store where the owner and cobbler could be seen over his shoe form mending the soles of shoes and work boots. His bald head was prominent and he smiled and waved as they rode by. There were two new churches, their steeples dominating over the rooftops of the homes. The news racks displayed three papers—the *Manistique Herald*, *Pioneer Tribune* and *Courier*.

As they rode across the old wooden bridge that crossed the Manistique River they rounded the corner and Lily saw the addition of a new saloon. It was a two-story building covered in red tarpaper. Standing out front were several Indian men and other rough looking men with disheveled clothes. They lined the wooden sidewalk holding mugs of beer and smoking cigars or pipes. Some of them spit tobacco juice into the dirt. She noticed the sign above the door, which read "Majestic." There were also two new buildings housing a grocery store and feed store.

They rounded the corner to take the final road home and passed the Ravenwood. Lily noticed May sitting on the front porch talking to a tall and handsome man. Lily hesitated a moment, then decided she would not let her father influence her acquaintances any longer. She smiled and waved at May as they passed and May returned an excited wave. Preacher Tom just scowled at her but he didn't say a word to Lily. Lily was no longer the giggling little girl she had been when she left Manistique. Now she was a mature young woman with a mind of her own.

May was so excited to see Lily go by. If she only knew how that feeling of excitement would diminish into sorrow by the next day. She hoped that now her brother and this woman could somehow be together and try to make a happy life for themselves. May told her friend who Lily was and told him the story of Lily and John's love, and how they had always been pulled in opposite directions. The man was impressed with the love May had for her brother and her wish for a romantic happy ending for the two ill-fated lovers. He was finding a lot of things impressive about May. Jacob had only known her for six months but she was always on his mind.

Lily unpacked her belongs, shared a quiet dinner with her father and turned in early. She was tired from her long journey and tomorrow would be the first time in three years she'd seen John Horn. She planned to rise early, pack a picnic lunch and ride her horse up into the woods to meet John Horn at Weber's spring. She felt no need to tell her father where she was going. She was no longer a little girl and she vowed to herself that she would not let him come between them again. He could not send her away again. She curled up in her bed and imagined John Horn's arms around her, holding her until she slept.

Lily rose with the rising sun. The birds gathered outside her window, twittering their wake-up songs. She packed her lunch, said goodbye to the housekeeper her father had hired and walked outside to greet the day. The morning dew clung to blades of grass, teardrops left by the angels. The daffodils, crocus and tulips were up in the yard. She could already feel the warmth of the rising sun. It was going to be a glorious day even if it was still crisp. Her horse whinnied his greeting as Lily scratched between his ears and kissed his nose. She saddled him and he galloped off, displaying her proudly on his back.

# Rendezvous at Weber's Spring

Weber's spring was a little slough off the Duck Creek. It was a sanctuary for birds, whitetail deer, sand hill cranes, beaver, otter and any other critter that happened along for a drink of water. You had to walk down a slight ravine to reach the natural beauty of it. As Lily made her way down the slope her breath caught in her throat as her eyes beheld John Horn. He was waiting patiently, sitting at the water's edge, his horse standing off to the side. The sun held the position of noon, causing the water to reflect like a piece of glass.

Her heart skipped a beat as he turned his head in her direction. Even before his horse whinnied he sensed her presence. She stood still and for a moment John thought she was an apparition. Her youthful face had taken on a vibrant glow of beauty. He didn't think it was possible for her to be even more beautiful than he remembered her. Her eyes sparkled with that blue-green spark as the corner of her mouth slightly curled upward. Her hair hung past her waist, the color of sweet flaxen. Her body had filled out to that of a voluptuous woman.

Lily did not take her eyes off him as she slowly made her way toward him. The steps he took toward her were like the steps of a mesmerized baby. He could hear the roar of his chest pounding as his heart longed to once again become connected with hers. He silently thanked his gods for the gift they had bestowed upon him. His life was finally complete.

When they stood before each other their arms automatically reached out for the other's as they became joined in each other's spirit like the mixing of water, limestone and clay. They both knew at that moment that even when they were split apart by everyday life, they would always be joined one and only to each other. They were finally in the one place they were destined by fate to be, in each other's arms.

Lily's upturned face was nose to nose with John's as their eyes met in the unity of love. Their lips met with the heat of a roaring fire. Their mouths opened to each other as the sweet taste of honey sated their taste buds and filled them. The heat of their bodies burned like a white-hot branding iron. They were consumed with a deafening roar as their passion discharged like gunpowder. Lily moaned with an unfamiliar feeling as she felt shivers on her neck and a hot flow of coals descending to the warmth of her womanhood.

John could hear his heart pounding, bouncing off the surrounding trees, glancing off the water, only to echo through the silent forest again and again. He wanted nothing more than to fill her body with his manhood. He wanted to finally taste the sweet nectar of her silken body, to feel the tender softness of her against his naked skin. His hardness pressed against the inside curve of her thighs. His manhood wanted to gently teach her the ways of love. *Is it too soon?* he thought.

He knew she was innocent and reason finally won over him, convincing him the time and place had to be perfect for both of them.

Separating himself from her he murmured, "Lily, we mustn't, we mustn't get carried off in our passion."

With a surprised look on her face Lily spoke through bated breath. "But I love you, John Horn, I want you to love me."

"I do love you, Lily, with all my heart and more, but we need to be smart about this, what would your father say?"

"Damn my father!"

John was shocked by Lily's outburst. He never thought she would ever say anything bad about her father. To hear her curse the preacher only made it worse. "Lily, please. He's still your father and I have to respect that. I know it's hard for you to understand but I must have his approval."

A tear dropped unto Lily's cheek as she looked into John's eyes with the look of a wounded fawn. She turned from him and walked toward the water's edge. She bent to pick up a flat stone and sent it skipping across the top of the water. A mallard duck and drake feeding on the other side skidded across the water, moving to a safer area. John silently walked up behind her and placed his arms around her, feeling the rise and fall of her breast. He wondered how long he could resist her.

They stood together, her resting her back against his chest, feeling his brawn. He nuzzled her ear as she whispered, "I missed you so much, John Horn."

"I missed you too, my love, more than I thought I could endure."

They watched as a doe walked cautiously out of the brush, taking a drink while her timid fawn made its way on wobbly legs. The spots were large, signifying a newborn that was less than two weeks old. It stumbled at the water's edge, comically catching itself from a fall. The doe nudged her nose into the butt of the fawn, encouraging it to move along and drink. She stood guard, flicking her tail. The fawn drank and moseyed off behind its mother, taking the same trail they had just emerged from.

The sound of Lily's giggle was like a melody to John's ears. How he had missed this little girl who was no longer a little girl, but a woman! Taking her hand he led her to a shaded spot under a pine tree. He grabbed a blanket off the back of his horse as he walked by. Spreading it out on the ground he gently began to tug her down to sit beside him. Lily chuckled and pulled her hand away, teasing him as she had when they were children.

"I've brought us a picnic lunch, John Horn."

She dashed off, scurrying up the ravine as sure-footed as an Indian scout. She decided to bring her horse down for a drink and get her acquainted with John's horse. They made their way back down the ravine; Lily grabbed the picnic basket as her horse scampered off toward the water's edge to take in a long swallow of the cool water.

John's horse sauntered over to nudge the mare, playfully nipping at her neck as she drank.

While Lily unpacked the fried chicken, some leftover potato salad and fresh bread, John leaned back against the tree, not believing she was actually there with him. The smell of pan-fried chicken wafted to the tip of his nose as he savored the aroma that reminded him of Mrs. Roxbury. It was his favorite and it had been on the table every Sunday that he could remember with her. The sweetness of the meat mixed with a breading of cornmeal, flour and seasoning simmering in a cast-iron pan of hot grease was always tantalizing. He was licking his lips by the time Lily handed him a plump chicken leg.

Lily tittered melodiously as John chomped into the tender meat and smacked his lips with pleasure. The potato salad was a special family recipe of her father's housekeeper. Red skinned potatoes, boiled eggs, wild leeks with a creamy mixture of butter, cream and mustard paste. The bread, still warm, was sweetened with fresh butter. The tang on John's taste buds couldn't have been finer.

They enjoyed their picnic lunch as John told Lily about his life in the lumber camp and his daily duties. The land lookers would search the forest for stands of good trees, some up to six feet in diameter and over seventy feet to the first limb. Shanty boys in gangs of three would cut down the trees with cross cut saws, some made for a two-man team. The limbs were severed with a double bitted ax sharpened to perfection. The logs were then loaded unto wooden sleds drawn by workhorses or oxen and taken to the riverbank. There, the lumberjacks used cant hooks to roll the logs or to drag them to the riverbank with chains. Each log would be marked on the end with a hammer; various log marks of the lumber companies were used. A log scaler measured each log, estimating how many board feet of each tree would be sacrificed to the cycle. The men worked from daylight to dark.

The logs would await their fate along the riverbank through the winter. When springtime finally arrived a pile pole would be used to push the logs into the river, crashing onto the thin ice being broken up by the thaw. The river hogs would take over from there, using peaveys to maneuver the logs, breaking up the logjams so the logs could float freely down the river to the mills in town. It was a dangerous job and the river hogs were a breed of men not only strong but strong willed. They were highly skilled like acrobats at a circus, sure-footed with a well-concentrated balancing act. They wore calked boots fitted with tiny spikes to keep their grip on the logs. It was a tense, dangerous job and they had to be aware of their surroundings at all times. They had to be the best there was.

John also told Lily about the camp foreman, Paul Knuth, and his wife Nelly, who was a camp cook. In the summertime Nelly would ride down the river on a cook shanty to deliver the noon meal to the lumberjacks. The shanty was a raft made of cedar logs for flotation. It was equipped with a cast iron potbellied stove which she used to prepare the meals. She would always make a stop at Cole's Landing along the river to visit with her sister.

There was also a cook's helper named Arvo Lyyski, a Finlander who originated from the South Republic area. There were times when the men would complain about the tough meat that he served them. It never failed, when they complained he would stomp into the eating area set up with long wooden tables and benches with a look on his face only a unique Finlander can give. He carried two large pots with him and he would bang them together to get the men's undivided attention.

He spoke in his native tongue but it translated to, "I hear ya don' like the meat. Ya think it's tough? If ya got teeth, use 'em, if ya ain't got 'em, get 'em!" He would then turn and stalk off back into the kitchen as the men grumbled, pissing and moaning at the still-tough meat.

Lily loved to hear John tell his stories. He was animated and made them come alive with his many expressions. They spent the afternoon sharing stories, talking over old times in Mackinaw City and finally making plans for their future. Lily was adamant about not letting her father stand in their way. They wanted to marry and have children. John told her about Bittenear and Lost Acres and promised to take her to meet him. John was already saving his money, along with the rest of his inheritance from Mrs. Roxbury, and soon he would have the amount he needed to build them a fine home along the Manistique River.

The afternoon was gone before they knew it and with only a few hours left of daylight, Lily knew she had to make her way back home. John worried about her riding alone in the woods but he knew as well as she did that she was connected to nature in the same way he was. There was no real danger of her being accosted along the trail back to town. John did worry about the wild animals but was reassured when Lily showed him the shotgun strapped to the side of her saddle.

"That's my girl!"

They said their goodbyes until the next time they would meet. Lily refused to let her emotions allow the tears to start flowing. She knew this was the only way until they could have better. John held her in a warm embrace, kissed her rosebud pouting lips and watched until she was out of sight. He couldn't believe they were finally together, even though they would be separated by the miles from Lost Acres to Manistique, thirty-six miles that felt like thirty-six thousand. Again he heard her delightful farewell whispered as soft as the powder on butterfly wings— "I love you, John Horn."

# THE BITTERSWEET TOMORROWS

As Lily rode into town the streets were unusually quiet. For some reason she felt an uneasiness stirring within her, an ominous feeling of dread she could not shake as she made her way down the road that would take her home. As she neared Ravenwood she noticed a group of people standing on the porch. It was May, Doctor Walker, Jake and Sarah. Some of the other girls were sitting on a porch swing. All the women were crying but May and Sarah were especially racked with grief. Lily's heart plunged to the pit of her stomach, feeling as if someone had slammed a fist into her insides.

She slowed her horse, walking her into the yard. Slowly descending she caught some of the words spoken by Doctor Walker, "She was too weak to fight it off, the croup took her."

May spotted Lily as she hesitantly made her way up the front porch, joining the bereaved group. Her face was ashen not knowing what to expect, whom they were talking about. She thought it was one of the girls who worked there, but why on earth would Jake and Sarah be there? Sarah let out another woefully choking cry as Jake rushed to comfort her.

Lily, looking to May for answers, said, "May, what is it? Is someone sick?"

Tearfully May told Lily that baby Rebekha had died just a few hours earlier. She had to explain that Korina's twins, Jeremiah and Rebekha had been adopted by the barren parents. May could hardly contain herself and Lily took her in her arms to try and comfort her. How sad. How devastating. How cruel.

Lily couldn't believe that she had just spent an entire afternoon happier than she'd been in so many lost years, only to arrive home to the cruelty of death stalking to the bed of a tiny helpless two-year-old baby, clutching the life from her as she slept. She silently questioned her faith in God but knew the blame was misdirected. Her sympathy went out to Jake and Sarah, not really being able to feel what they were feeling at this moment. Her empathy was inadequate.

She noticed then that one of the girls was holding a black-haired little boy on her lap. His angelic face was clueless to the desolation around him. He fidgeted with a locket hanging around the neck of the girl who held him. He squirmed, wanting to be let down to go to his mother. His actions showed anxiety but he would not understand for many years that his twin sister was dead. As a twin he would always feel the unforgivable void of losing half of himself.

Lily held May and wept for the baby girl she had never known, for the parents who had been given the sweet precious gift of two babies, only to lose one of them so soon and for May, the woman with the sincerity of an angel. Lily could only imagine how she would feel if she were ever to have John Horn's child only to lose it in this same way. She wanted so frantically to be able to make it all be unreal. She knew her desperation was hopeless.

Doctor Walker placed his hand on Jake's shoulder, saying, "I'll take you home."

Jake almost had to carry his inconsolable wife to the carriage as Doctor Walker picked up little Jeremiah, toting him along. As he walked by Lily she looked once again at the innocence of youth, that angelic face of a little boy. Jeremiah reached out his tiny hand and with a Cupid smile said, "Where Bekha?"

Lily's whole body ached with sorrow as the lump in her throat hardened once again to a painful compression. She could not contain the tears as they welled and fell in a steady crescendo down her cheeks. She had turned the corner of the road home with the anticipation of telling May of her happiness and had come upon a scene that would affect her for a very long time to come.

Turning to May she croaked, "I'm so sorry for them, May. I feel so helpless; I wish I knew what to do."

May understandingly answered, "There is nothing any of us can do now. God must have needed an angel. Our lives were fortunate to have her for the short time we did. It will take time but Sarah is a strong woman with great faith, she'll come to deal with this in her own way."

"Oh May, I came here with such joy in my heart, having been to see John. I never dreamed I would come upon this sadness beyond words."

"Don't stop being happy for yourself, Lily, you and John have been apart for too long. We'll talk tomorrow; you will attend Rebekha's service, won't you?"

"Oh yes, I'll come."

Lily watched as May walked almost ethereal up the stairs and into the front door of Ravenwood. Lily took the reins of her horse and slowly walked toward home. Her heart went out to Jake and Sarah and her thoughts held an image of the sweet little boy, Jeremiah.

When she entered her house Lily went to the library which her father used as an office. She was still shaken and needed his support. When she opened the door a crack she could tell he was deep in thought, preparing his sermon for Sunday. She wished their relationship could be as it was when she was a child, but she knew there was the good beginnings of a wall separating them.

"Father, did you hear about Jake and Sarah's little girl?"

The rage showed in Preacher Tom's eyes as he hollered across the room, "Where have you been all day, Lily? You didn't ask if you could go anywhere."

Lily was stunned at her father's burst of ill temper. She wasn't accustomed to it and she didn't like it. Stepping further into the dimly lit room with a cozy fire burning in the fireplace she felt the chill of reprisal.

"Did you hear me, Lily? Where were you today?"

Lily stammered, "I—I went up into the—the woods, I brought John Horn a picnic lunch. Father, did you hear me? Do you know what happened to Jake and Sarah's baby? She died, Father, the baby died, don't you even care?"

If the look of anger on her father's face were a hand it would have reached across the room and placed a stinging slap on her cheek.

He furiously bellowed, "Lily, I forbid you to see that half-breed good for nothing— "

"Father," Lily shouted back, "I am an adult. As much as I respect you I will not have you telling me whom I can and cannot see!"

Preacher Tom glared at his daughter.

"What has become of you, Father? Why is your heart so hardened?"

Lily and Preacher Tom both knew they were at a standoff. Lily could not understand her father at all. Preacher Tom could not stand the thought of losing his only daughter. He realized she was a grown woman now but he couldn't stand the thought of her losing her innocence to a no-good Indian lumberjack. He wanted better for her and the battle constantly raged within him. What could he possibly do to make her understand?

Lily quietly walked over near her father and gently placed her hand on his shoulder. "Father, I love you, we mustn't argue this way. I'm a grown woman now and I have to find my own way in this world. I love John Horn. He's the only one I've ever loved. We want to marry and have children. He respects me and would never do anything I did not want him to do. Why can't you understand that?"

Preacher Tom's shoulders slouched in defeat. He was a tired and emotionally worn man. "You're all I have, Lily, don't you understand that? If you are to stay in my home, I must insist that you abide by my rules and I forbid you to see that man. Do you understand, Lily?"

"I understand, Father."

"I want you to stay away from the Indian whore's brothel, too."

Lily bit her bottom lip as it began to tremble with the anger brewing inside her. She knew an argument would be futile. She turned and walked out of the room and away from the father she no longer knew from her youth.

Lily slept fitfully, sweet dreams of John Horn intermingled with the terror of her father catching them together and tearing them apart. Terrible images of her father attacking and killing John Horn kept her tossing and turning into the wee hours. With the dawning sun she arose and prepared to attend the funeral service of a precious baby.

She met May in front of Ravenwood and they rode together with the other girls across town and to the little cemetery on the hill. The cemetery overlooked the Tannery, a tiny community lined with company houses for the men who were employed tanning hides. A shallow grave had already been dug and a Catholic priest stood with a large group of mourners.

Lily, May and the other girls joined the group as the priest began his eulogy for the little angel who God had called back home. He ended with "Yea, tho I walk through the valley…" Some quietly wept over the tiny pine box as it was lowered into the ground. Others stood in shocked silence, listening to the grief-stricken wails of Sarah. The gravestone was already in place in the shape of a baby lamb, symbolizing innocence. The undertaker kept a supply on hand for the many babies who died too soon. Chipped into the stone was "Baby Rebekha. 1895."

Everyone offered their condolences to Jake and Sarah as the service ended. Turning to leave, Lily noted a flaw in the texture of the stone. The sun shone upon it just right and there appeared to be a teardrop under the lamb's eye. She could envision God and the angels crying for the people who had loved baby Rebekha. Baby Rebekha now had angel wings.

-Baby Rebekha's headstone-

# A Love Story

Lily and John continued to meet at Weber's spring. Lily had told him about that first confrontation with her father. The relationship they had as father and daughter continued to dwindle away. Lily's love for John Horn far outweighed the strained relationship she had with her father. She would let nothing come between her and John Horn. Never.

The two lovers could not meet every week and sometimes went for several months without seeing each other. John would always send word through Uncle Semo and Lily would faithfully pack a lunch, saddle her horse and ride off out of town using the well-ridden road and winding narrow pathway to arrive at Weber's spring. In the winter months they would meet at Lost Acres where they spent the afternoons talking with Bittenear. When John was in town they would meet at Ravenwood. John had his own room there and they were thankful for the privacy. Lily suspected her father knew but he never again voiced an opinion or demanded any restraints. He was not the same man. Now he was glum and moody, and it showed in his interaction with the parishioners. People commented but never questioned his morose attitude.

With each meeting it became more difficult for the two lovers to resist each other. The passion emitting between them sent off sparks in all directions, like those that came with placing an ax to a whetstone. After a year of trying to resist each other, they sealed their pact of love with the joining of their naked bodies. They had always been one in spirit and now they were one in spirit and body. Their love could not possibly be any stronger.

Even when they were separated, they were joined as mercury is as it spills from a broken thermometer. Split in two with a knife, it always finds its way back to the one solidity it is. It can never be separated; it consistently slides across any surface toward the whole in unification. They breathed as one, their hearts beat as one, their natural state of being was one.

When Lily looked into John Horn's eyes they were soft with compassion. She could walk into them and be filled with a warmness that would melt her soul as it reached out to him. His lips were sensuous and searching, speaking intimate whispers that made her insides shake with desire. His fingers were slow and gentle, touching her lips and face, running smoothly through her flowing hair. His hands were strong, boldly bringing sparks to the surface of her velvety skin, sparks that were drawn from the hot burning embers within her.

John Horn's arms reached out to her with a craving that could only be sated when she filled the space between them, an empty space that only she was destined to fill. He would touch her, quietly drawing her body and her very being into his. She would arc toward him and her pulsing ache would turn to desire. His body moved with the tender serenity of a feather which made Lily tremble with passion. She would be filled with his manhood, the part of his body that made him a man because of its hardness and strength, and its need to be tamed.

He filled the most private part of her body, the part that was nestled between her legs as they wrapped around him. Her intimacy, warm and wet, cried out to be filled. He reached the very depths of an all-consuming fire that raged through Lily's every vein. His explosion would ripple through him to join with her sweet ecstasy of a passionate union. Lily looked into John Horn's eyes and knew love.

Behind Lily's eyes hid the mystery of herself. She endlessly searched her mind for John Horn's face so their eyes could lock with inner beauty. Her lips, holding a hint of a smile at the corner of her mouth, kissed his eyelids, brushing his cheek, opening slightly so her tongue could glance across his lips, and then softly nibble on the lobe of his ear.

Lily's fingers searched with the need to touch John Horn everywhere. She felt the texture of his hair as it glided through her fingers. She would grasp his strong shoulders as her breath escaped her in gasps that became moans of pleasure. Her hands reached out in the darkness with a longing to hold John Horn's hand in hers. She felt the need to stroke his manhood to life. She would caress his back, feeling the broadness that covered her with protection. Her arms with a tender desire would bring him to her, never to let him go. There was an empty pain and only he could fill the void.

Lily's touch only cared about the drawing power they shared. She touched his soul, his spirit, leaving her with a calm that would last forever. Her touch released his senses as John Horn drank in her sweet nectar, the scent of her perfume on the back of her neck, between her breasts and on her inner thighs. The vanilla and honeysuckle that lingered in her hair filled him. The scent of the lotion she used to soften her skin was the scent of jasmine.

Lily's body would rise above her, drifting in the wisp of a breeze. It would come gently to him and lay with him. Every nerve of her being would be brought to the surface. Her nerves developed extremities that would clutch into every inch of his skin. She brought John Horn into her existence through the love and passion he had released in her. She would straddle him with her legs drawn up on his sides and cling to the yearning to be his.

Her womanhood was hot and burning for the ecstasy of being filled by him. Her wetness readied her for each union. His loins cried out to hers, already known to each other. He had captured her innocence and they would crave the pleasure they knew was there. Lily would bring him to her, to enter into the quivering heat of her intimacy. There, he would know he had found the way into the depths of a burning desire.

Lily's love came from an awareness she had always known. A love that could allow them each to say, "I love you." But the words did not need to be spoken, they had already been. They had only been parted by fate and by destiny they were together again, to love for eternity.

Lily's explosion would smolder inside her, waiting to be set free, wanting to mingle with his. Her insides would shake with a delight in feeling the ripples of a climax that pierced through her like a lightening bolt, melting her being. Her passion became an unquenchable appetite for more and after her screams of delight were subdued the rapture would smolder in her eyes.

# SPRING OF 1897

John had ridden into Manistique early in the morning. He had errands to run before the start up of a new seasonal log run. He needed a new pair of boots; his spikes were wearing down and that could be dangerous. The one thing that could be fatal was to lose his footing while riding the logs down river. Not only was there the danger of frigid water, but the chance of drowning in the waters of the Manistique River.

John planned to visit briefly with Uncle Semo and Moonwater. It had been two months since he'd seen them both and that long since he'd seen Lily. She, of course, was always on his mind but today he had a special errand in mind. There was a new jeweler in town and he had already decided to purchase a wedding band for Lily. If he didn't see her today he would leave word with Uncle Semo for her to meet him tomorrow. He had made the decision to quit working for the Chicago Lumbering Company at the end of the summer's log run. He was twenty-four and it was time for him to settle in with a wife and family.

He was deep in thought as he entered the company store where he was met with a smile from one of the busy clerks. He was disappointed to learn that the new supply of boots wasn't due until the end of the week. His worn calked boots would have to do him until then. He would have to be extra cautious with his maneuvering on the logs. He met Jake as he walked out the door and offered his condolences for his lose of Rebekah. He learned that Sarah was finally beginning to accept it and was very overprotective of Jeremiah.

He made his stop at the jeweler and picked out a fine gold band, so small it could fit a child but meant only to be worn on the left hand of the petite Lily Abrams. The jeweler congratulated him. John left, smiling and whistling a merry tune, sitting tall on the back of his horse as he rode through the streets of Manistique toward Ravenwood.

John made his way across town to see Moonwater. She had great news for him as he walked into the dining area. Her beau had proposed to her and they planned to be married and move to Illinois. She already had a buyer for Ravenwood and the papers would be drawn up next month. Her face was aglow as she introduced John to her soon to be husband. Offering his hand he gave his sister his blessings.

"It seems that we all have good news to tell," John said, smiling.

May knew the look of a Cheshire cat when her brother was hiding a secret. She also knew he always told his secrets to her. "What is it, John, what is your secret today?"

"I just came from the jeweler. I've bought a wedding band and as soon as I see her I'm going to ask Lily to be my wife."

"John, that's wonderful!" Moonwater grabbed her brother around the neck and gave him a hearty hug.

"Oh John, I'm so happy for you, I know you and Lily will be so happy and have a long life together with many children. I want to be an auntie many times!"

"Have you seen Lily around?"

"No," Moonwater offered, "but I heard she's been sick. I think it's just a sniffle or an upset stomach, nothing serious."

Seeing that John looked worried anyway she quickly said, "I'm sure it's nothing, she usually stops by every day, she'll come see me when she's feeling better."

"Yes, you're most likely right, May."

"Can you stay for dinner, John?"

"Thanks, but I have to get back. We're starting a new log run in the morning and I have to sharpen my tools yet. When you see Lily will you tell her to meet me at Lost Acres next Tuesday?"

"Yes, I'll be sure to tell her. She'll be so happy to hear from you."

John shook Jacob's hand, welcoming him as his future brother-in-law, and told him how happy he was for him and Moonwater. He left with no doubt that he was a good man and would be a good husband to his sister.

As John hoisted himself onto his stallion's back he gave Moonwater a look of reproof and said, "You be good now and don't tell Lily my secret."

"John," she squawked, "you know I wouldn't do that!"

"Take care, sister, I love you."

"I love you too, brother."

Moonwater watched until John was nearly out of sight, sitting astride his horse with the pride of Chippewa blood running through his veins. His long black hair whipped in the wind. When he got to the end of the road, before he took the turn for town he stopped, turned his horse slightly to the side, and held his arm high above him. The sun was beginning to set and he stood in silhouette against the reddened sky. Moonwater could envision an ancient warrior leaving his people, taking a journey to speak to the elders about peace and security of the tribal members. Her pride for her brother was eternal.

# Spring of a New Dawn

Lily woke for the first time in a week with a calm stomach. She had been sick to her stomach and vomiting every morning. The other signs were there too. She had looked in a book Suzanne had given to her when they were at school. It was a book that told about the changes that happened in a young girl's body when she was on the threshold of being considered a woman. It described the cycles and changes a woman's body goes through. She already knew about the monthly bleeding; she had begun that when she was fifteen.

That was not what Lily had been looking for and found in the book. Her breasts were tender, she had missed the last two months of her bleeding cycle and the queasiness in her stomach every morning was a sure sign. Lily was going to have a baby. Her emotions swirled like a sandstorm. She was happy. She was sad. She was afraid. She was excited. She was nervous. She was serene. She was going to have a baby! She was going to be a mother.

She knew she had to tell John Horn as soon as possible. She knew he would be so happy. They had already talked about getting married and now there was little time left to do it. She had already calculated and the baby would be born in November, in seven months. She decided to walk down to Ravenwood to see if May had heard from him. She would not say anything to her until she could tell John Horn he was going to be a father.

After talking to May she learned she had just missed John the previous day and was so happy to learn they would be meeting at one of their special places in the wilderness in just four more days. She went home with a renewed spirit, deciding on the way back that she would not say a word to her father. She knew that she and John Horn would be married soon and she would save the news until after their vows were spoken and she became Lily Horn, Mrs. John Horn.

Early Tuesday morning, a chilly overcast day, Lily rode to Lost Acres, stopping momentarily at Weber's spring. The ground was still slightly frozen and there were still small chunks of ice on the pond. The wild flowers were starting to force their way up through the ground with green shoots fighting their way to freedom, searching for the warmth of the sun that would open their buds to form fresh brilliant petals. A mallard duck flew over. Not wanting to land on the water, it settled into a clump of weeds in the marshy area. Bright green buds were starting to pop out on the hardwood trees. A doe, heavy with her unborn fawn walked by, dipping its head for a drink of fresh water. Lily marveled at all the new life awakening around her. She loved the springtime. She held her hands on her belly and whispered to her unborn child, "Your father and I are going to love you with all our hearts, little one."

Lily made her way up the slope and mounted her faithful mare. She rode down the path that would take her to the clearing of Lost Acres. The smell of fresh spring air and new pine needles filled her nostrils as she delighted in the start of a new season. Bittenear saw her approaching the shack and marveled at her beauty. Her blonde hair hung past her waist, long wisps lilting up into the air as the occasional breeze caught it and brought it to life. Her peach-toned skin had a fresh glow. A shot of blush reached her cheeks as she smiled and waved at seeing him. Her eyes glowed with the radiance of a woman in love.

"Bittenear, how are you on this glorious day?"

"It is that. How are you, Lily? Happy to see you."

"I see that John isn't here yet, I guess I'll pull up a stump and wait for him."

Bittenear helped her with the stump and offered, "Just boiled some water, got some of that new choclate powder to mix in it, have some?"

Lily and Bittenear sipped their hot drink and chatted, waiting for John Horn. He was never late. When he said he'd meet her he always showed up a short time after Lily arrived. In the two years they had been meeting, he had never been late, not once. The apprehension tightened every muscle in Lily's body. She did not want to worry and make herself sick with her wandering thoughts of all the possibilities for John being late.

With each story that Bittenear told, and he had so many, the sun, although hidden behind an overcast sky, ticking like a clock, made its way further down to its place of setting for the day. John Horn did not come. By now Lily was in a state of panic and Bittenear feared the worst. Catching a movement on the trail leading to his property, Bittenear saw a man approaching. He recognized him as one of the men John had brought for a visit a few times. Bittenear saw the dread of a bearer of bad news and did not want to believe what he already knew in his heart. He had had a vision the night before and knew that John Horn's fate had been set by the gods of the river.

Lily stood, her face drained of color, knowing too that the man was bringing bad news. She looked to Bittenear, compelling him to stop the man from opening his mouth and saying the words she could already hear. She felt the force of her soul being ripped from her, the soul that was joined with John Horn's was being shredded apart before her very eyes and she could do nothing to stop it. She felt his soul being separated from hers, ripping and shredding with the force of a tree splitting apart after being struck by lightening. She heard the pain-filled cry as it cracked open, shards of wood separating. She reached out, trying to pull John Horn back to her being.

Lily's heart screamed with agony as the man finally spoke the fateful words. "John Horn is dead."

"Nooooo!" Lily screamed. Her horse spooked, running off behind the shack. Her scream reverberated off the trees, silencing the sounds of the forest. Her scream swirled around and around, bouncing off branches and rocks, rolling through the ravines and valleys, bouncing and banging back to Lily's mouth only to begin again. "Nooooooo!"

The newness of springtime sensed the starkness of death as every living thing in the forest hushed, hushed, hushed. The only sound now was Lily's heart, rending sobs of sorrow. She crumbled into a heap onto the forest ground, curled into a childlike ball and wept. Bittenear did not touch her; he knew she had to grieve in her own way. The gods would give her strength.

Bittenear walked off to the side of the shack and the lumberjack told him what had happened that morning.

The river had broken up early with an occasional chunk of ice flowing by. The logs that were piled on the riverbank were being pushed into the river at a steady pace. The river hogs were working furiously and skillfully to maneuver the logs down river. At a bend in the river the logs jammed. John Horn was working the logjam. He had commented earlier about the worn spikes on the soles of his boots. He had to wait for a new pair to come in.

As he worked with the peavey to move the logs, part of the jam shifted and the sudden shift of weight caused John to lose his footing, the momentum tossing him into the icy water. He could survive the frigid temperature if one of the men got to him in time, but as his head bobbed up to the surface, his arms reaching out to grab onto anything, the logs shifted again, sending the butt end of a log into the side of his head. It knocked him unconscious and he immediately sank again into the icy grasp of the Manistique River. The grip of death held him under and he knew nothing. Time had stopped and John Horn was dead.

They found him a short distance down river. His body, frozen in the perpetual stiffness of death, was pulled from the water and buried on that very spot along the river. He lived and died a brave man. The men carved his name into a wooden makeshift cross—John Horn, April 1897. They bowed their heads and said a solemn prayer over his shallow grave. "The Lord is my shepherd, I shall not want…"

# THE WOMEN

Bittenear tucked Lily into the extra bunk that John Horn had slept in for nearly two years. He had scooped her up into his arms and carried the limp and ragged girl who had just that morning been vibrant with life. He tucked the quilt snuggly around her, knowing she would sleep nestled in the warmth of John's embrace with the scent of his body still on the blanket. She was despondent, inconsolable and kept mumbling something about a baby. Bittenear guessed what it was. John Horn had left his legacy behind and never knew it. He would never again know the joy of Lily and experience the pleasure of being a husband and father.

With the end of one life, a new one began. He had played his part in the mysterious cycle of life. Now he lay nestled in the arms of Mother Earth. Sister Sun would blink at him each new morning and Sister Moon would wink at him each night. Brother Sky would protect him from any restless spirits. He was one with nature and died how he lived, a brave and honest man. The only thing wrong, was he had died too young.

Bittenear rode to town early, leading Lily's horse with Lily sitting like a stone upon its back. She had emptied herself of every tear. She could cry no more. Her state of mind was lost to the crushing blows that had smashed her spirit the day before. The glow was gone from her cheeks; even her hair appeared to have lost its vibrancy, hanging limp against

161

her back. Her eyes stared into an unseen unfamiliar distant land. The blue-green sparkle had lost its luster. She heard him whisper to her as they rode by Weber's spring, *I love you Lily Abrams.*

When they arrived in town she refused to go home. She had to be with May when Bittenear told her about John. She knew that May's life would be forever changed, just as hers would. May had been so happy about her marriage proposal and the sale of Ravenwood. She was looking forward to her life in Illinois. She was happy leaving knowing John and Lily would be together forever. All of her happiness was about to be smashed to smithereens.

As they rode up to the front porch of Ravenwood they saw May on the porch swing, as still as the calm before a storm. She didn't move. She didn't come forward in her usual way of greeting. She didn't smile. Lily met her eyes and knew that May already knew about her brother. The town must have been buzzing with the devastating news already. It was always a tragedy when anyone died and it affected most of the townspeople in the same way.

Bittenear held Lily to his chest and whispered, "Be strong, Lily, be strong for John Horn and his baby." He turned and rode away.

Lily walked like a vacant apparition up the steps and sat down beside May. May reached out and took Lily's hand and they grieved in silence, knowing exactly what the other was feeling. Words were not needed, only the love and support of each other, the only two women in John Horn's life, the only two women he had loved with an undying love. He was gone but his love would always be a part of Moonwater and Lily.

When May finally spoke it was to say, "He loved you so, Lily, he had bought you a wedding ring when he was in town last, he was going to ask you to marry him. I don't have to keep his secret now."

Lily felt the warmth of John Horn's arms around her as she embraced his sister's rendition of his last words.

Lily shared her secret. "I'm having his baby, May. I will always have him with me. He will always live in my heart but his life will go on in his child. I was going to tell him, he would have been so proud."

Lily and May held each other, new tears falling silently on each other's shoulders. Lily's thoughts went to Weber's spring and the days they had spent there along the water's edge. *I'll always love you, John Horn.*

# CRY OF THE WOOD LILY

There was nothing left in Manistique for either of them. It was too painful to stay. May had already packed her belongings, waiting for her future husband to take her to her new life. She had finalized the sale of Ravenwood and the new owners had hung a new sign, changing the name to the Klondike. Most of the girls would stay on, already liking the new owners, two brothers from Wisconsin. She had already said goodbye to Lily, knowing of her plan to leave for Pennsylvania. Lily had broken the news of carrying John Horn's child and her father had rejected her, sending her away without his blessing. They had promised to keep in touch and May planned to visit when the baby was born. She would say goodbye to Uncle Semo on the dock.

Lily had packed her belongings, said goodbye to May and Uncle Semo and rode one last time up into the woods to say her goodbyes to Bittenear. He would take her to John Horn's grave where she could say her final farewell to the man she loved with every beat of her heart.

When they came upon his grave Lily noted the serene setting along the riverbank and knew in her heart that John Horn would rest peacefully here. The lonely cross of wood stood serenely by itself amidst the pines. The birds chirped their songs with the accompanying melody of the water's flowing rhythm. A shaft of sunlight shone down between the branches of the towering pines, its subdued light enhancing the lone grave.

Bittenear stood back to let Lily say her goodbyes. He watched as she placed a kiss on the wooden cross that marked the grave of a fallen lumberjack. She picked some nearby wild violets and, placing them atop the mound of earth, bent her knees to be nearer to him and said, "Goodbye, John Horn, I will love you forever." She wept.

Their horses lead them back along the trail to Lost Acres and Bittenear and Lily embraced with a somber farewell. She knew she would probably never see him again. He knew he would never get her face out of his mind. She was as special to him as a daughter would be.

"Take care of yerself, Lily."

"You take care too, Bittenear. You will always be special to me. I will never forget you. Thank you for being John Horn's friend and thank you for being as special to me as a father."

He watched until she was nearly out of sight. She stopped, turning her horse to the side, and held her arm up above her head in a final Indian farewell. The glaring beams of the sun fell on her flowing hair and placed the luster back into it. She was too far away for him to see but he knew at that moment the sparkle was placed back into her eyes too. He and Semo had talked once of the girl with the moon in her eye. She had the special touch of the ancestors.

Lily stopped briefly at Weber's spring to feel the last embrace of John Horn. She stood by the water's edge listening for his voice in the breeze. She felt his sensuous touch on her cheek. She could not bring herself to speak it aloud but her thoughts whispered within her, *I love you, John Horn*. Her eyes welled with new tears and fell in droplets onto the ground. She left behind her a trail of tears and when each one touched the earth she was not aware of the gods of nature as each tear brought forth a sprout, pushing its way toward the sunlight. Each lush green sprout continued to grow, leaves unraveling until it reached a height of about eight inches. At the top of each stalk a pure white bud opened, bringing forth a wood lily with a braided pistil of yellow, as yellow as Lily's hair. Each one swaying in the breeze whispered, "I love you, John Horn."

-Wood Lily (Trillium) in the Manistique Forest-

# DREAMING AND FAMILY HISTORY

The morning after I spoke with Emma Simms, I woke up still fresh with a montage of dreams. The pictures that had made a collage in my psyche were not sent to my dream catcher for expulsion. I wanted to laze there and revel in the wonder of the wafting images of a time long gone, to cherish the many faces that swirled around like autumn leaves. The never-ending love shared by John Horn and Lily had filled the honeycomb of my dreams and tasted sweet with the morning sun.

No love story could have been more fulfilling than the images that had come to life in my slumber. My dreams had played like a scene from a grand Broadway play. Each character deserved a standing ovation for capturing my undivided attention through the night. Stricken with awe as each new act was performed I was uplifted into a realm dominated by reincarnation, or as close as I could come to believing in it.

Emma Simms had provided me with photographs and names of her ancestors. The imaginations of my poetry provided what could have been. The grave with the little lamb headstone was so much a part of my childhood that I had gone there again in my dream state and was finally able to know baby Rebekha. The journey back in time with the sprigs of information in my subconscious mind had given me the ultimate journey through the streets of Manistique in the late 1800s.

Listening to old-timers talk of their youth makes for an entertaining night at the cinema of sleep imagery. To be guided through the night while floating along on the end of a vivid red ribbon, one wishes to remain asleep for as long as possible. Many places I had grown up around became places of laughter, tears and love for people I had brought to life during my reverie. As a young girl I could stand on the hilltop of the original cemetery on the hill in Manistique and overlook my home, the Tannery. In my dream state the Tannery had been a busy place on the outskirts of town, lined with houses for the men who used hemlock to tan hides in the 1800s.

Almost every Sunday we would go on a family ride, taking all the back roads going to my dad's camp in the Manistique Forest. We would cross the Bear Creek Bridge, the CC Bridge and the Duck Creek Bridge. We would always make Dad stop before he drove over the old Duck Creek Bridge, afraid the car would crash through it and we would fall into the creek. We called it the Rickety Bridge. Always, of course, in many of our trips to camp, we would visit the grave of John Horn.

-Duck Creek Bridge in the Early 1960s-

# -Another View of the Duck Creek Bridge-

The investment my dad had made in the forty and half a forty when he was nineteen had been proudly named God's Lost Acres. It is an actual place where I fit into the surrounding natural beauty of the woods. The little creek that flowed next to the camp always provided a nearby place to catch frogs. We were warned not to drink the water but we always did, first skimming off whatever seen and unseen things floated on the surface.

John Horn

-God's Lost Acres-

-God's Lost Acres in the Wintertime-

# -Steam Heat Behind God's Lost Acres-

In my dream, Bittenear had joined the medley of characters and had taken on the attributes of my dad, Bud Weber. Dad used to go on the rendezvous with a group of mountain men from Illinois, living in a teepee and taking part in shooting contests and hatchet throws. He had cut teepee poles for many years for the other mountain men. When he refused to take money after measuring, cutting and peeling many poles, the men presented him with a set of buckskin leggings and a buckskin jacket. The precious gift has been his pride for many years now.

My dad added to his special wardrobe by hand crafting pouches for gunpowder and pellets used for his long arm muzzleloader. He collected animal bones and porcupine quills, crafting necklaces and charms. He picked up carcasses of raccoons, tanning the hides with a salt mixture and designing coonskin caps. He went back in time in his own extraordinary way and gained the title of Bittenear at a rendezvous.

-My Dad Proudly Portraying Chief Bittenear-

While sitting in a tavern, one of the longtime mountain men decided that my dad needed an Indian name. Without warning and with no special treatment and with a total lack of tenderness, the man walked up and bit my dad on the ear until the blood ran down his neck. He nipped a piece of his ear lobe off, spitting in unto the floor, dubbing him Chief Bittenear.

My dad has a special old trunk where he stores his buckskins, hats and other paraphernalia of the mountain man he is. Years ago he would dress up, tour the schools for my brothers or nieces, or head out of town to Munising and walk into a tavern where he would be greeted with mixed emotions. Some people thought he was a kook; some respected his unique peculiar way, especially in the Upper Peninsula of Michigan.

Many will remember him and laughingly tell a story about a particular bone whistle the old timer would always carry. There was nothing hand crafted about it; it was the penile bone of a raccoon. He carried them in various sizes on a necklace looped around his neck. Invariably, many people would ask if they could have one. On one particular adventure in Munising he stopped down the road where he skillfully cut the penile bone from a dead raccoon. He had it in his pocket with the bloody skin and hide still attached. Before he gave it to his unsuspecting admirer, he asked, "Do you want a fresh one?" Their reply was always in the affirmative. When someone yelped in surprise, dad would drink his Budweiser and chuckle.

Mind you, the animal was already dead when this was done. My dad in no way is disrespectful of the little critters that grace our land. He believes in the old ways of the Indians—only take what you need and use everything it provides. My dad is so in tune with nature he should have lived in the 1800s. I've always thought he was born 100 years too late. My dad is seventy-eight years old and gramps is ninety-nine. That is a legacy of which I can stand proud.

My dad is so unique that when the character Bittenear entered my dreams along with John Horn, Lily and the many others who made an appearance, I knew it was because my dad holds such a special place in my heart. I am proud to have him for a father and honored to know Chief Bittenear.

Just before the last couple of curves in the road to God's Lost Acres is a little slough on the right hand side, filling up from the Duck Creek. When going to camp Dad would always stop so we kids could sneak down the slope, hoping to see a doe and fawn. A natural spring flowed into the slough and we would always get down on our hands and knees and take a long refreshing drink.

It was a special place for us, a tranquil scene in the middle of the woods. I'm not sure when it became known as Weber's spring but my dad made a driftwood sign he hung on a tree. One end was larger than the other was and it looked like an arrow pointing the way to our secluded sanctuary. An old boot hung on a branch near it, seeming to proclaim the remains of a long-dead lumberjack. Weber's spring is so familiar to me there's no doubt why it became a part of my dream. I relived the intimacy of this spot through the placement of John Horn and Lily meeting there for their shared picnic lunches.

One of my gramps' brothers owned a saloon in Manistique years ago, thus setting the stage for its inclusion in my dream. It's funny how the conscious and subconscious mind can grab at bits of our memory like flecks of lint and cause the formation of a delusion that seems so real. Landmarks were remembered with dignity and discussed over and over, and the Ossawinamakee Hotel was one place that was remembered with grandeur. The Indian name has pride written through it that makes one flattered to have known the overwhelming feeling of maybe having stood on the steps of the magnificent building that had adorned the main street in Manistique.

My great grandparents emigrated from Bavaria, coming to Manistique on a schooner where they were greeted by an Indian wrapped in a colorful blanket, thought to be Ossawinamakee. The brothers helped build the existing St. Francis de Sales Catholic Church in Manistique. It's no wonder that Sebastian filtered into the countryside of my dream. The home I lived in for eleven years was a block away from the dock in Manistique. It happened to be one of the houses one of the original Webers made their home back in the late 1800s.

The Jamestown Slough formed when the Manistique River was

damned up during the lumberjack days, allowing for the logs to be brought downriver. Growing up in the Tannery, the slough provided us with a favorite fishing and swimming hole. Many winter days were spent ice fishing and clearing the snow for ice-skating. When the Manistique River was allowed to take its natural course back in the late 1900s, it resulted in the slough becoming void of any water. Now, with the thick new growth of trees and brush there are still the remaining well-worn ruts of an old logging trail where for years the horse-drawn carts and logging sleighs crossed many times hauling loads of virgin white pine.

I know with each of my footprints in all my old stomping grounds that I have walked the same streets, wood trails and riverbanks that the early settlers did. I have sat in the woods in the same spots the lumberjacks sat to eat their lunch. I have drunk from the same creeks and streams. Many of those long-dead lumberjacks were responsible for the ambiance surrounding me. Many of their voices whispered in the breezes. Many of their spirits may have watched me run and play as a child. I would like to believe that one of them was John Horn.

Whenever I walk in the woods I am caressed with the warmth of emanating life. The serene forest is a comforting force of nature. I'm convinced that in days long gone there really was a Lily who frequented the spots now familiar to me. I can envision her embedded into the serenity of the woodlands.

-Samantha Mitchell (Lily) Amidst the Wood Lilies-

# EMMA SIMMS, 2003

I contacted Emma Simms after I had replayed my night dreams in my mind. I offered to take her to John Horn's grave, the grave of not only a long-dead lumberjack, but also her great grandfather. We met in town and I drove to my dad's where he stood on his step in all his glory, like the greeter Ossawinamakee did in the old days. Dressed in his skins he had taken on his character of Bittenear. He was honored to meet John Horn's granddaughter and even more honored to be our guide.

We take his truck up into the Manistique River Forest. After crossing the Bear Creek Bridge we turn left at the Y, bumping over the gravel road with a small slough on our right. Painted turtles sun themselves on the logs, wood ducks float aimlessly. A doe stands in the marsh, a spotted fawn frolics beside her. Up a slight incline and around a curve, we come upon the CC Bridge. Dad stops the truck in the middle of the bridge where we all get out and stand near the railing, watching the steady flow of the Manistique River, envisioning the thousands of logs that had been driven down it, hearing the calls of the river hogs. Emma carries her camera, basking in the wonder of its beauty, snapping pictures.

Resuming our ride we gracefully weave our way down the winding road as it becomes narrower. We pass the old road that was once the entrance to gramps' camp. A partridge walks in front of us trailed by her scurrying covey of eight little ones. Dad slows until they are out of harm's way. The thankful mother stops, drumming her wings against her chest, the unmistakable reverberation echoing through the woods.

Another fork in the road and we take a right, passing the back entrance to the Depot, another Weber camp designed from old railroad ties and a front door with the Bunny Bread bunny on it. It had hung for years at Barney's Grocery in Manistique. We come upon a bad spot in the road. It is an area that washes out with water covering it from the Duck Creek. Even driving through the washout, Dad knows where the holes are underneath and skillfully drives through it. Rounding another curve we come upon the Duck Creek Bridge, the Rickety Bridge, again stopping so Emma can snap pictures. Two more doe and a yearling stand in the tree line. Their white tails flicking their warning, then turning, they bound off into the safety of the trees.

Several grandiose sand hill cranes fly over, their wingspan reaching to an extraordinary length of eight feet. We can hear their distinctive call as they fade into the skyline. Once nearly extinct, their numbers are steadily growing. Dad tells Emma about his misadventure of once walking through the woods and happening on a nest of resting baby cranes.

Without warning he was attacked by the mother. She swooped down, hitting him with the defensive force of her legs, slamming him to the ground. Once he realized what was happening he scrambled up and started running through the woods to safety. The crane raised itself into the air, made a wide circle and again plunged down with her force, slamming him down onto the ground again. She was definitely on a mission to protect her young. He got to his feet again and ran stumbling and crashing through the woods, as fast and far away as he could.

We continue on, the old truck winds around corners, climbing another incline in the road. Then comes the clearing. The devastation, the raped trees all cut down. A clear cut. It is a scene that breaks my heart every time I see it. It's how they replenish the forest but the desolation of it is a stark reminder of the striking beauty that once was there. All the majesty of the red pine and jack pine along the Manistique

River on the road leading to God's Lost Acres is now a graveyard of crudely cut stumps, life hacked away. Emma is stunned for the first time and Dad and I are bewildered for the hundredth time.

Rounding a corner where there is another fork in the road, there, on our left hangs a new sign for Weber's spring. Dad stops so we can walk down the slope and stand to revel in its beauty. A serene alcove in the woods. It is a remarkable place, where John Horn may or may not have spent long afternoons with Lily. We all stand in silence, each in our own thoughts, as a pair of mourning doves land on a branch overhanging the pond. They coo, making us aware of the aura of John and Lily that surrounds us.

Walking up the slope, Emma turns to savor the scenery. I see her tear up, as she no doubt imagines her great grandparents in a compelling love story, just as I had dreamed the night before. Even though she takes photographs the photograph in her mind will never leave her.

We snake around a couple more twists in the road and reach the beginning of the property line of God's Lost Acres. It is very distinct now because of the remaining pines standing like royalty, a reminder of the virgin pines that graced the forest with their natural beauty. We pass the entrance to Virgin Ridge, my brothers' camp, and not fifty steps away, God's Lost Acres. Off to the left is my share of the property, which I have affectionately named Camp Bittenear. It's nothing more than a rough foundation sitting there surrounded by a bounty of trees. I don't even have my sign up but in my heart that is my special portion of a man who is his own legend, my dad.

Dad, with the expertise of an Indian guide, takes Emma and me into the woods. It's not the same trail from my childhood, now it's been butchered of trees and the marked branches used for landmarks fell with the trees. We don't have to cross the river anymore; we're approaching from the backside of the grave site. Dad turns us around in circles a couple times, he himself not so familiar anymore with the way in. He always says he never gets lost in the woods; he just gets turned around for a couple days.

We finally come upon the place in the woods that greets us with subdued serenity. There in the midst of the landscape is the cement gravestone with the brass plaque—John Horn, April 1897. The grave lot is framed with a wooden fence. There are faded plastic cemetery flowers and a few wild flowers naturally growing there, and of course, the wood lilies.

I stoop to clean the weeds and dead leaves from the grave. I look up to see Emma fighting back tears. Everyone coming to John Horn's grave displays a mixture of emotions but no one has more right to that emotion than Emma. She has heard the family history of her great grandfather being buried along the Manistique River but never dreamed of actually standing near it one day.

Through a tear-strangled voice Emma says, "I can't thank you enough, Bud."

"No thanks needed, Emma."

Emma looks to me, saying, "Two poems could not have been more appropriate for what I've seen today. Thank you for bringing my grandparents to life in your words."

"Thank you, Emma, I'm just glad you're able to finally be here to see it for yourself."

A redheaded woodpecker hammering, chisels into a tree, the blue jay sounds his call, a soft breeze begins to stir as the pine needles dance with calm movement, but all becomes hushed in the forest as the delicate wood lilies sway and the whisper is faint but we all hear it: *I love you, John Horn.*

Dad clears his throat, and we all bow our heads and pray, "The Lord is my Shepherd, I shall not want... "

-John Horn's Grave-